Leslie (

slie Charteris was born in Singapore on 12 May
07. In 1919 he moved to England with his mother
d brother and attended Rossall School in Lancashire
fore moving on to Cambridge University. His studies
re came to a halt when a publisher accepted his first
vel. His third book, entitled *Meet – The Tiger!*, was
written when he was twenty years old and published in
928. It introduced the world to Simon Templar, a.k.a.
he Saint.

He continued to write about the Saint up until 1983,
when the last book, *Salvage for the Saint*, was published
by Hodder & Stoughton. The books, which have been
translated into over twenty languages, have sold over 40
million copies around the world. They've inspired
fifteen feature films, three TV series, ten radio series
and a comic strip that was written by Charteris and
syndicated around the world for over a decade.

Leslie Charteris enjoyed travelling, but settled for
ng periods in Hollywood, Florida, and finally in
rey, England. In 1992 he was awarded the Cartier
Diamond Dagger in recognition of a lifetime of achieve-
ment. He died the following year.

LESLIE CHARTERIS

Señor Saint

Series Editor: Ian Dickerson

MULHOLLAND
BOOKS

HODDER

First published in Great Britain in 1959 by Hodder & Stoughton

This paperback edition first published in 2014 by Mulholland Books
An imprint of Hodder & Stoughton
An Hachette UK company

1

A CIP catalogue record for this title is available from the British Library

Paperback ISBN 978 1 444 76650 9
eBook ISBN 978 1 444 76651 6

Typeset by Hewer Text UK Ltd, Edinburgh
Printed and bound by Clays Ltd, St Ives plc

Hodder & Stoughton policy is to use papers that are natural, renewable and recyclable products and made from wood grown in sustainable forests. The logging and manufacturing processes are expected to conform to the environmental regulations of the country of origin.

Hodder & Stoughton Ltd
338 Euston Road
London NW1 3BH

www.hodder.co.uk

CONTENTS

INTRODUCTION

So here's how Simon Templar changed my life.

I was fourteen, in my first year of Catholic High school in a dying post-industrial city in Massachusetts. I was a Good Boy. Went to church, studied hard, joined student council – the lot. Folks used the word 'clever' around me. My moral framework was set, my worldview ordered. The future was good grades, a fine college, some solid middle class job.

Then, on a shelf in the local library, I met the Saint.

I'd had a little pulp experience – swung with Tarzan, travelled the world with Doc Savage – but those heroes were too large for real life. Jungle men and genetic prodigies. But Simon Templar? Simon was just very, very . . . what's the word . . .

. . . clever.

The Saint was my introduction to the Trickster Hero. His ability to win, not by force, but by manipulating men and systems to destroy themselves fascinated me. It began my lifelong obsession with unravelling every system I encountered in life. What were its rules? How did it work? How could it be broken? I could never be Tarzan, or Doc Savage, but a smart man with a bit of nerve, oh, he could be Simon Templar.

My interest in fiction suddenly changed to pulp and detectives, anti-heroes and crime. Heroes who didn't just break the rules, but broke them because it was the right thing to do. Heroes who had complex morals in a complex, grey world. I could suddenly acknowledge something that had been haunting me – the secret sense that the world was not, in fact, ordered or fair or predictable. Fate is fickle and cruel. It will devour the brave and foil the virtuous . . .

. . . but the clever hero, he can ride Fate. He can survive in a grey world.

I did go to college – but in a foreign city, to see a bit of the world. Then my hobby for stand-up comedy overtook my career in physics (don't ask) and I went on the road. Ten years of nightclubs, grifters, gamblers, mobbed-up doormen, nights where the club owner offered to pay you in cocaine rather than cash. I travelled the world; picked up enough Spanish, French and German to order drinks; learned my wines and, more importantly, my scotches; got my nose broken in a barfight and broke a few myself. I learned that in every bad spot, there was always a man big enough to put you down. But if you were a bit faster, a bit more charming, a bit more clever like Simon Templar, you'd come out of it okay.

Eventually I turned to writing. I started in sitcoms (most comedians make that transition) but when I moved to one-hour dramas and movies, I made a very fine career out of writing the Trickster Hero. My heroes always won because they were smarter. They always had a plan. They did the right thing, even if it was the wrong way. There was a niche for this writing, and not a lot of screenwriters filling it. Simon Templar gave me my career.

This culminated, of course, with *Leverage*, the TV show I created and ran. Four thieves led by one honest man, Nate Ford. By now, of course, Nate's come to admit he's not exactly an honest man anymore. He's the Mastermind, the vicious bastard who'll risk his neck to save a kid or bankrupt a corrupt millionaire. Nate may be working-class Boston Irish, but I'd like to think in the vast fictional universe he and

Simon Templar butted heads once or twice, and bought each other drinks on more than one occasion.

The theme of *Leverage* was spoken aloud by our thief Parker (and yes, that's a direct homage) in the first season. Confronted by a confused Honest Citizen, she shrugs and says 'Sometimes Bad Guys are the only Good Guys you get.' *Leverage* is a direct descendant of the Simon Templar stories. While I can't imagine the stories will change your life they way they did mine, I'm sure you'll enjoy watching Simon Templar travel the world, helping the helpless, righting wrongs, ripping off the rich, and being generally very clever indeed.

John Rogers

THE PEARLS OF PEACE

I

Before the idea becomes too firmly established that Simon Templar (or, as it usually seems easier to call him, the Saint) never bothered to steal anything of which the value could be expressed in less than six figures, I want to tell here the story of the most trivial robbery he ever committed.

The popular conception of the meanest theft that can be committed is epitomized in the cliché of 'stealing pennies from a blind man'. Yet that, almost literally, is what the Saint once did. And he is perhaps prouder of it than of any other larceny in a list which long ago assumed the dimensions of an epic.

The Saint has been called by quite a thesaurus of romantic names, of which 'The Robin Hood of Modern Crime' and 'The Twentieth Century's Brightest Buccaneer' are probably the hardest worked. By public officials obligated to restrain his self-appointed and self-administered kind of justice, and by malefactors upon whom it had been exercised, he was described by an even more definitive glossary of terms which cannot be quoted in a publication available to the general public. To himself he was only an adventurer born in the wrong age, a cavalier cheated out of his sword, a private robbed of his black flag, with a few inconvenient ideals which had changed over the years in detail but never in principle. But by whatever adjectives you choose to delineate him, and with whatever you care to make of his motives, the sober arithmetical record certainly makes him, statistically, one of the greatest robbers of all time. Estimates of the total loot which at one time or another passed through his hands, as made by mathematically-minded students of these stories, vary in their net amount: his expenses were always high, and his interpretation of a tithe to charity invariably generous. But by any system of calculation, they run comfortably into the millions.

Such a result should surprise nobody. Simon Templar liked big adventures, and in big affairs there is usually big money involved, this being the sordid state of incentives in our day and age.

But the Saint's greatness was that he could be just as interested in small matters when they seemed big enough to him. And that is what the incident I am referring to was about.

This happened around the town of La Paz, which in Spanish means only 'Peace'.

2

La Paz lies near the southern tip of the peninsula of Baja California, 'Lower California' in English – a long narrow leg of land which stretches down from the southern border of California and the United States. On account of the peculiarly ineradicable obsession of American statesmen with abstract lines of latitude and longitude as boundaries, instead of more intelligible geographic or ideographic frontiers, which accepted the ridiculous 38th-parallel partition of Korea as naturally as the quaint geometrical shape of most American state lines, this protuberance was blandly excluded from the deal which brought California into the Union, although topographically it is as obviously a proper part of California as its name implies. There is in technical fact a link of dry land south of the border connecting Baja California with the mainland of Mexico, but there is no practical transportation across it, no civilized way from one to the other without passing through the United States: for all the rest of its length, the Gulf of Lower California, or the Sea of Cortez as the Mexicans know it, thrusts a hundred miles and more of deep water between the two.

Thus like an almost amputated limb, Baja California hangs in the edge of the Pacific, bound to Mexico by nationality, to California by what terrestrial ligaments it has, nourished by neither and an anomaly to both. The highway artery leaps boldly across to Tijuana and contrives to keep going south to Ensenada, bearing a fair flow of tourist blood; but then almost at once it is a mere dusty trickle of an almost impassable road, navigable only to rugged venturers in jeeps, which meanders through scorched and barren waste lands for hundreds of empty miles to La Paz, which is the end of the line.

La Paz is a port of long defunct importance, seeming to survive mainly because its inhabitants have nowhere else to go. But that was not always true. Here in the fine natural harbour, once, toplofty Spanish galleons came to anchor, and bearded soldier-monks peered hungrily at the rocky shore, eager to convert the heathen with *pax vobiscums* or bonfires, but with some leaning towards the latter, and always with an eye to the mundane treasures that could be heisted from the pagans in exchange for a sizzling dose of salvation. But the gold of that region, though it was there and is still there, was too hard to extract for their voracious appetite, and they sailed on towards the richer promise of the north. Others, however, who came later and stayed, discovered treasure of another kind under the pellucid warm blue waters nearby: once upon a time, the pearl fisheries of La Paz were world famous, far surpassing the product of the South Pacific oyster beds which most people think of in that connection today.

And that is what this story began to be about.

'It was the Japs,' Jocelyn Ormond said. 'They put something in the water that killed off all the oysters. They were all up and down this coast just before the war, pretending to be fishermen, but really they were taking soundings and mapping our fortifications and getting ready for all kinds of sabotage. Like that.'

'I know,' said the Saint lazily. 'And every one of them had a Leica in his pocket and an admiral's uniform in his duffel bag. Some of it's probably true. But can you tell me how destroying the Mexican pearl industry would help their war plans against the United States? Or do you think it was some weird Oriental way of putting a spell on everything connected with pearls, like for instance Pearl Harbor?'

'You're kidding,' she said sulkily. 'The oysters *did* die. You can't get away from that.'

When they were introduced by a joint acquaintance he had a puzzling feeling that they had met somewhere before. After a while he realized that they had – but it had never been in the flesh. She was a type. She was the half-disrobed siren on the jacket of a certain type of paper-bound fiction. She was the girl in the phony-tough school of detective stories, the girl that the grotesque private eye with the unpaid rent and the bottle of cheap whisky in his desk drawer is always running into, who throws her thighs and breasts at him and responds like hot jelly to his simian virility. She had all the standard equipment – the auburn hair, the bedroom eyes, the fabulous mammary glands, the clothes that clung suggestively to her figure, the husky voice, the full moist lips that looked as if they would respond lecherously enough to satisfy any addict of that style of writing – although the Saint hadn't yet sampled them. He couldn't somehow make himself feel like the type of cut-rate Casanova who should have been cast opposite her. He couldn't shake off a sense of unreality about her perfect embodiment of the legendary super-floozy. But there was no doubt that she was sensational, and in a cautious way he was fascinated.

He knew that other men had been less backward. She was Mrs Ormond now, but she had discarded Ormond some time ago in Reno. Before Ormond, there had been another, a man with the earthy name of Ned Yarn. It was Ned Yarn whose resuscitated ghost was with them now, intangibly.

'I mean,' she said, 'they were all supposed to have died – until I got that letter from Ned.'

Simon went to the rail of the balcony which indiscreetly connected their rooms, and gazed out over the harbour and the ugly outlines of La Paz, softened now by the glamour of night lights. They were sitting outside to escape from the sweltering stuffiness of their rooms, the soiled shabbiness of the furniture and decoration, and the sight of the giant cockroaches which shared their tenancy. For such reasons as that, and because your chronicler does not want to be sued for libel, the hotel they were staying at must be nameless.

'Let me see it again,' he said.

She took the worn sheet of paper from her purse and gave it to him, and he held it up to read it by the light from inside the room.

Dear Joss,

    I know you will be surprised to hear from me now, but I had no heart to write when I could only make excuses which you wouldn't believe. You were quite right to divorce me. But now I have found the pearls I came for. I can pay everyone back, and perhaps make everything all right with you too.

    The only thing is, it may be delicate to handle. Say nothing to anyone, but send somebody you can trust who knows pearls and doesn't mind taking a chance. Or come yourself. Whoever comes, go to the 'Cantina de las Flores' in La Paz and ask for Consuelo. She will bring him to me. I won't let you down this time.   *Always your*

                                 Ned

The writing was awkward and straggly, up hill and down dale, the long letters overlapping between lines.

'Is this his writing?' Simon asked.

'It wasn't always that bad. Maybe he was drunk when he wrote it. Now that we're here, I wonder why I came on this wild-goose chase.' She stared at the anaemic residue in her glass. 'Fix me another slug, Saint.'

He went back into the room, fished melting ice cubes from

the warming water in the pitcher, and poured Peter Dawson over them. That was how she took it, and it never seemed to affect her much. Another characteristic that was strictly from literature.

'That letter is dated over five months ago,' he said. 'Did it take all that time to reach you, or did you only just decide to do something about it?'

'Both,' she said. 'I didn't get it for a long time – I was moving around, and it was just lucky that people kept forwarding it. And when I got it, I didn't know whether to believe it, or what to do. If I hadn't met you, I mightn't ever have done anything about it. But you know about jewels.'

'And I'm notorious for taking chances.'

'And I like you.'

He smiled into her slumbrous eyes, handing her the re-filled glass, and sat down again in the other chair, stretching his long legs.

'You liked Ormond when you married him, I suppose,' he said. 'What was the mistake in that?'

'He was a rich old man, but I thought he needed me. I found out that all he wanted was my body.'

'It sounds like a reasonable ambition.'

'But he wanted a bird in a gilded cage. To keep me in purdah, like a sultan. He didn't want to go places and do things. He'd give me presents, but he wouldn't let me have a penny of my own to spend.'

'An obvious square,' said the Saint. 'But you fixed him. What about Ned?'

'I was very young then, just a small-town girl trying to crash Hollywood and making doughnut money as an extra. And it was during the war, and he was young too, and strong and healthy, and that Navy uniform did something for him. It happened to a lot of girls . . . And then the war was over, and I woke up, and he was just a working diver, a sort of submerged mechanic, earning a mechanic's wages and going nowhere except under docks and bridges.'

Simon nodded, leaning back with his freebooter's profile turned up impersonally to the stars. He had heard all this before, of course, but he wanted to hear it once again, to be sure he had heard it all.

'That's all this Tiltman wanted,' she said. 'A good working diver. Percival Tiltman – what a name! I should have known he was a phony, with that name, and his old-school-tie British accent. But he knew where the richest oyster bed of all was, and it was one that the Japs had missed somehow, and he had some real pearls to prove it . . . Of course, he needed money too – for equipment, and a boat, and bribes. Mostly for bribes. That should have been the tip-off, all by itself.'

'I don't know,' said the Saint. 'I can believe that the Mexican Government might take a dim view of foreigners coming down and walking off with their pearls.'

'Well, anyway, he got it.'

'It was about ten thousand dollars, wasn't it?'

'Exactly eleven thousand. Most of it was from my friends – people I'd known in the studios. Ned's best friend put some in. And twenty-five hundred was my own savings, from what Ned had sent me while he was overseas.'

'And Ned and Brother Tiltman took off with it all in cash?'

'All of it. And that's the last anyone heard of them – until I got that letter.'

'How hard did you try to find him?'

'What could I do? I didn't have an address. Ned was going to write to me when he got down here. He never did.'

'There's an American vice-consul.'

'We tried that, after a while. He never heard of them.'

'How about the police?'

'I wrote to them. They took three weeks to answer, and

then they just said they had no information. Perhaps some of the money *was* used for bribes, at that.'

'I mean the American police. Didn't anyone make a complaint?'

'How could I? And make myself the wife of a runaway crook? Our friends were very nice about it. They were sorry for me. I've never felt so humiliated. But it was all too obvious. Ned and Tiltman had just taken our money and run off with it. It wasn't even worth anybody's while to come down here and try to trace them. They'd had too long a start. By the time we realized what they'd done, they could have been anywhere in South America – or anywhere in the world, for that matter. I just waited till Ned had been gone a year, and divorced him as quietly as I could, for desertion.'

'But,' said the Saint, 'it looks now as if he'd been here all the time, after all.'

Mrs Ormond swished the Scotch around over the ice in her glass with a practised rotary motion, brooding over it sullenly.

'Perhaps he came back. Perhaps he spent all his share of the money, and now he thinks he can promote some more with the same gag. Who knows?'

'It was nearly ten years ago when he disappeared, wasn't it?' said the Saint. 'If he got half the loot, he's lived on less than six hundred a year. That's really making it last. If he was going to try for more, why would he leave it so long? And why did he disappear when he did, without any kind of word?'

'Don't ask me,' she said. 'You're the detective. All I know is, there's something fishy about it. That's why I wouldn't have come here alone. You'd better be careful. I hope you're smarter than he is.'

Simon raised an eyebrow.

'When this started, you gave the impression that he was almost boringly simple.'

'That's what everyone thought. But look what he did. He must have had us all fooled. You can't believe anything he says.'

'I'm not exactly notorious for buying wooden nickels – or plasticine pearls. I'll keep my guard up.'

'Do that in more ways than one. I told you, he was a very husky guy. And he could be plenty tough.'

'I can be tough too, sometimes.'

She eyed him long and appraisingly.

'Come here,' she said, in her throatiest voice.

He unfolded himself languidly and stood beside her.

'No, don't tower over me. Come down to my level.'

He squatted good humouredly on his heels, close to her chair.

'You look strong,' she murmured, 'in a lean leathery way. But I never found out how far it went. That's why I like you. You're different. Most men are in such a hurry to show me.'

Her hand felt his arm, sliding up under his short sleeve. Her eyes widened a little, and became soft and dreamy. The hand slid up to his shoulder, and the tip of her tongue touched her parted lips.

Simon Templar grinned, and stood up.

'I'm strong enough,' he said. 'And I'll be very careful.'

3

He had already located the Cantina de las Flores – had, in fact, been inside it earlier in the evening. It was a small and dingy bistro in a back street of unromantic odours, and the only flowers in its vicinity were those which were painted in garish colours on the sign over the door. An unshaven bartender in a dirty shirt had informed him that Consuelo would not be there until ten. It was only a few minutes after that hour when the Saint strolled towards it again.

He would probably have been less than human if he had not thought more about Jocelyn Ormond than about Consuelo on the way over. Consuelo was only a name; but Mrs Ormond was not easy to forget.

He tried to rationalize his reaction to her, and couldn't do it. According to all tradition, there should have been no problem. She not only had all the physical attributes, in extravagant abundance, but she knew every line in the script, in all its cereal ripeness. The dumbest private eye on the newsstands could have taken his cue and helped himself to the offering. Yet the Saint found a perverse pleasure in pretending to be blandly unconscious of the routine, in acting as if her incredible voluptuousness left him only amused. Which was an outright glandular lie.

He shook his head. Maybe he was just getting too old inside . . .

The bar, which had been drably deserted when he was there before, was now starting to jump. There were a dozen and a half cash customers, a few obviously local citizens but a majority with the heterogeneous look of seamen from visiting freighters – a sterling and salty clientele, no doubt, but somewhat less than elegant. There were also half a dozen girls, who seemed to function occasionally as waitresses, but who also obviously offered more general hospitality and comradeship. Instead of the atmospheric obbligato of guitars with which no Hollywood producer could have resisted backgrounding such a set, an enormous juke box blared deafening orchestrations out of its rococo edifice of plastic panels behind which coloured lights flowed and blended like delirious rainbows, a dazzling and stentorian witness to the irresistible march of North American culture.

Simon went to the counter and ordered a beer. The bartender, only a few hours more unshaven and a few hours dirtier than at their first meeting, looked at him curiously as he poured it.

'You are the *señor* who was looking for Consuelo.'

'Is she here now?'

'I will tell her,' the man said.

Simon took his glass over to the juke box and stood reading the list of its musical offerings, toying with the faint hope that he might find a title which suggested that in exchange for a coin some slightly less earsplitting melody might be evoked.

'You were asking for me?' a voice said at his shoulder.

The Saint turned.

He turned slowly, because the quality of the voice had jolted him momentarily off balance. It was an amazing thing for a mere voice to do at any time and, against the strident din through which he had to hear it, it was almost incredible. Yet that was what it achieved without effort. It was the loveliest speaking voice he had ever heard. It had the pure tones of cellos and crystal bells in it, and yet it held a true warmth and a caress and a passion that made the untrammelled sexiness of Jocelyn Ormond's voice sound like a crude rasp. Just those few words of it stippled goose-pimples up his spine. He wanted the space of a breath to re-establish his equanimity before he saw the owner.

Then he saw her; and the goose-pimples tightened and chilled as if at a touch of icy air, and the jolt he had felt turned to a leaden numbness.

She could have been under thirty, but she was aged in the cruel way that women of her racial mixture, in that climate, will age. You could see Spanish blood in her, and Indian, and undoubtedly some African. Her figure might once have been enticingly ripe, but now it was overblown and mushy. Her black hair was lank and greasy, her nose broad and flat, her painted mouth coarse and thick. Even under a heavy layer of powder that was several shades too light, her complexion showed dark and horribly ravaged with pockmarks. She smiled, showing several gold teeth.

'I am Consuelo,' she said in that magical voice.

Somehow the Saint managed to keep all reaction out of his face, or hoped he did.

'I am looking for an American, a Señor Yarn,' he said. 'He wrote a letter saying that one should come here and ask for you.'

Her eyes flickered over him oddly.

'*Si*,' she said. 'I remember. I will take you to him. *Un momentito.*'

She went to the bar and spoke briefly to the bartender, who scowled and shrugged. She came back.

'Come.'

Simon put down his glass and went out with her.

The sidewalk was so narrow that there was barely room for them both, and when they met any other walkers there was a subtle contest of bluff to decide which party should give way.

'It was a long time ago that he told me to expect someone,' she said. 'Why did you take so long?'

'His letter took a long time. And there were other delays.'

'You have the letter with you?'

'It was not written to me. I was sent by the person to whom he wrote.'

Some instinct of delicacy compelled him to evade a more exact naming of the person. He said, cautiously: 'You know what it was about?'

'I know nothing.'

Her high heels clicked a tattoo of fast short steps, hobbled by a skirt that was too tight from hip to knee.

'I have never met Señor Yarn,' he said. 'What kind of a man is he?'

She stopped, looking up to search his face with a kind of vehement suddenness.

'He is a good man. The best I have ever known. I hope you are good for him!'

'I hope so too,' said the Saint gently.

They walked on, zigzagging through alleys that grew steadily narrower and darker and more noisome; but the Saint, whose sense of direction could be switched on like a recording machine, never lost track of a turn. The people who shared the streets with them became fewer and vaguer shadows. Life went indoors, and barricaded itself against the night behind shutters through which only an occasional streak of yellow light leaked out. It revealed itself only as a muffled grumbling voice, a sharp ripple of shrill laughter, the wail of a baby, the faint tinny sound of a cheap radio or gramophone; and against that dim sound-track the clatter of Consuelo's heels seemed to ring out like blows on an anvil. If the Saint had not stepped silently from incurable habit, he would have found himself doing it with a self-conscious impulse to minimize his intrusion. If he could conceivably have picked up Consuelo, or any of the other girls, in the Cantina de las Flores, without an introduction, and had found himself being led where he was for any other reason, he would have been tense with suspicion and wishing for the weight of a gun in his pocket. But he did not think he had anything to fear.

When she stopped, a faint tang of sea smells penetrating the hodge-podge of less natural aromas told his nostrils that they were near another part of the water-front. The shack that loomed beside them was different only in details of outline from the others around it – a shanty of crumbling plaster and decaying timbers, with a rambling roof line which could consist of nothing but an accumulation of innumerable inadequate repairs.

'Here,' she said.

She opened the cracked plank door, and Simon followed her in.

The whole house was only one little room. There was a brass bedstead against one wall, with a faded chintz curtain across the corner beside it which might have concealed some sort of sanitary facilities. In another corner, there was an ancient oil cooking stove, and a bare counter board with a chipped enamel basin. On shelves above the counter, there were cheap dishes and utensils, and a few canned foods. Clothing hung on hooks in the walls, between an assortment of innocuous lithographs pinned up according to some unguessable system of selection.

'Ned,' Consuelo said very clearly, 'I have brought the Americano you sent for.'

The man sat in the one big chair in the room. It was an overstuffed chair of old-fashioned shape, with a heavily patched slip cover, but he looked comfortable in it, as if he had used it a lot. He had untidy blond hair and a powerful frame, but the flesh on his big bones was soft and shrunken and unhealthy, although his skin had a good tan; and his clean cotton shirt and trousers hung loosely on him. His face had the cragginess of a skull, an impression which was accentuated by the shadows of the dark glasses he wore even though the only light was an oil lamp turned down so low that it gave no more illumination than a candle. He turned only his head.

'I was afraid no one was ever coming,' he said.

'My name is Templar,' said the Saint. 'I was sent by – the party you wrote to.'

'My wife,' the man said. 'You don't have to be tactful. Consuelo knows about her.'

'Your ex-wife,' said the Saint.

Ned Yarn sat still, and the dark lenses over his eyes were a mask.

'I guess I'd sort of expected that. How did she get it? Desertion, I suppose.'

'Yes.'

'Is she . . . ?'

'She was married again, to a man named Ormond.'

'I don't know him.'

'They're divorced now.'

'I see.' Yarn's bony fingers moved nervously. 'And you?'

'Just an acquaintance. Nothing more. What with changing her name, and changing her address several times, apparently your letter took a long time to find her. And then she didn't want to come here alone, and couldn't decide who else to trust. Now I seem to be it.'

'Sit down,' Ned Yarn said.

Simon sat on a plain wooden chair by the oilcloth-covered table. Yarn looked around and said: 'Do we have anything to drink, Consuelo?'

'Some tequila.'

She brought a half-empty bottle and three small jelly

glasses, and poured a little for each of them. She put one of the glasses on the edge of the table nearest to Yarn. Yarn stretched out his hand, touched the edge of the table, and slid his fingers along it until they closed on the glass.

'You must excuse me seeming so helpless,' he said harshly. 'But you see, I'm blind.'

4

The Saint lighted a cigarette, and put his lighter away very quietly. He glanced at Consuelo for a moment as she sat down slowly on the other wooden chair at the table, and then he looked at Ned Yarn again.

'I'm sorry,' he said. 'How long ago did that happen?'

'Almost as soon as I got here.' The other gave a kind of short two-toned grunt that might have been meant for a laugh. 'How much did she tell you about all this?'

'As much as she knows, I think.'

'I can figure what else she thinks. And what everybody else thinks. But you know as much now as I knew when I came down here with Tiltman. That's the truth, so help me.'

'I hope you'll tell me the rest.'

Yarn sipped his drink, and put it down without a grimace, as if he was completely inured to the vile taste.

'We flew down here from Tijuana, and I thought it was all on the level. A chance to make some big money legitimately – that is, if we weren't bothered about bribing a few Mexicans not to watch us too closely. I'm just a sucker, I guess, but I fell for it like all the others. I was even carrying the money myself. We checked in at a hotel, the Perla.'

'And yet the American vice-consul and the police couldn't find any trace of you. That seems like an obvious place for them to have started asking.'

'Tiltman registered for us both – only he didn't use our names. If you want to check up on me, ask if they've got a record of Thompson and Young. He told me that later.'

'How long did he play it straight?'

'We had dinner. Tiltman was supposed to have arranged for a boat before we left Los Angeles. I was all excited and raring to go, of course. I didn't even want to wait till morning to look it over. I wanted to see it that night. He tried to stall me a bit, and then he gave in. We set out walking from the hotel. He led me through all kinds of back streets – I haven't the faintest idea where. Presently, in one of the darkest of them, we came to a bar, and he said, "Let's stop in for a drink." '

'The Cantina de las Flores?'

'No. I didn't even know the name of it. But, anyway, we went in. We had a drink. And then, as calmly as anything, he said: "Look, Ned, I'm going to stop beating about the bush. There isn't any boat. There isn't any diving equipment – all that stuff we ordered sent down here from Los Angeles, I cancelled the order and got your money back." '

'And the great lost bed of pearl oysters?'

'He said: "That's just a rumour I heard when I was down here, sort of a local legend. But I don't know where it is, and nobody else does. It just gave me the idea for a good story to pick up a nice lot of money with. All that money you've got in your pocket," he said.'

'That must have called for another drink,' murmured the Saint.

'At first I thought he was kidding. But I soon knew he wasn't. He said: "I could've taken it from you tonight and left you holding the bag. But I like you, Ned, and I could use a partner. I've got tickets for both of us on a plane to Mazatlán. Let's split the money and go on and make a lot more like it." '

Simon barely touched his glass to his lips.

'And you said no?'

'I swear it. I told him he'd never get his hands on any of the money I had. I was taking it right back to Los Angeles, and I'd see what the police here could do about getting back the refund he'd gotten on the diving equipment. And I walked out.' Ned Yarn twisted his knuckles tensely together. 'I didn't get very far. He must have followed me and crept up behind me. Something hit me on the head, and I was out like a light. It's been lights out for me ever since.'

'The money was gone, of course.'

Yarn nodded. He said: 'You tell him, Consuelo.'

She said: 'I found him. It was just outside here. I was going to work. I thought he was drunk. Then I saw the blood. I could not leave him to die. I took him in my house. Then, when he did not get well quickly, I was afraid. I thought, if I call the police, they will say I did it to rob him. I sent for a doctor I know. Together we took care of him. He was sick for a long time. And then I could not turn him out, because he was blind.'

'And you've looked after him ever since,' said the Saint, and deliberately averted his eyes.

'I was glad to.' He heard only her voice. 'Because then I had fallen in love.'

And now the Saint understood at least a part of that strange story, with a fullness that left him for a little while without speech.

Ned Yarn had never seen Consuelo. He had met her only as a voice, a voice of indescribable sweetness, just as the Saint had first met her; but Ned Yarn had never been able to turn his eyes and have the mental vision that the voice created shattered by the sight of her coarse raddled face. And the woman who spoke with the voice had been kind to him in a way that fulfilled all the promise of its rich tenderness. Her figure would have been better then, and perhaps even her face less marred; and his fingers, when they clumsily explored her features, would not have been sensitive enough to trace them as they really were. They could easily have confirmed to him a picture that his imagination had already formed and was determined to believe. And in his perpetual darkness there could be no disillusion . . .

'Maybe you think I'm a bum,' Ned Yarn said. 'Maybe I am. But what could I do? I didn't have a penny, and I couldn't go more than a few steps by myself. Tiltman probably thought he'd killed me with that crack on the head. He might almost as well have. It was months before I really knew what was going on. And even then I still couldn't think straight, I guess.'

'You figured by that time everyone would have decided you'd run off with Tiltman and the money,' said the Saint.

'Even Joss. I couldn't blame her. I was just too ashamed to try to write and explain. I didn't think anyone would believe me. I guess I was wrong; but by the time I started to think it out properly, it was later still – that much more too late. And by then . . .' The premature lines in his face softened amazingly. 'By then I was in love too. I didn't really want to go back.'

Ash tumbled from the Saint's long-neglected cigarette as he put it to his mouth again.

'But you finally wrote to Jocelyn,' he said.

'I'm coming to that. After a while, I realized I couldn't go on for ever doing nothing but being sorry for myself, letting Consuelo keep me on the money she made as a waitress.'

From the matter-of-fact way Yarn said it, Simon knew that the man could never have had any idea of the kind of place she worked in. He was aware of the woman's eyes on him, but he gave no sign of it.

'Her doctor thought there might be a chance of getting my sight back if I could go to a first-class specialist,' Ned Yarn said. 'But that would cost plenty of money. And I couldn't go back to the States for treatment when it'd probably mean being put in jail. I needed even more money, to pay everybody back what I'd helped them to lose through Tiltman. I wanted to do that anyway. When I finally got my guts back, I knew that was what I had to do somehow – pay everyone off, and get my eyes fixed, and make a fresh start.'

'You still believed in that overlooked oyster bed?'

'It was the only chance I could think of. Eventually I talked Consuelo into helping me. She has a friend who's a fisherman, and he'd let us borrow his boat sometimes. We went out as often as we could. We searched all over, everywhere.'

'You went diving, when you were blind?'

'No, Consuelo did that. With a face mask. She can swim like a fish, she tells me. I just sat in the boat. And then, when at last she found oysters, I'd haul up the baskets she filled, and help her to open them. And as I wrote to Joss, we finally did it. We found those pearls!'

'The jackpot?' Simon asked.

Ned Yarn shook his head.

'I don't know. Quite a few, so far. Consuelo sold a few small ones, to get money to make us just a little more comfortable. And six months ago we bought a boat of our own, so we could go out more often. Of course she got practically nothing for them, because of the way she had to sell them. And she couldn't show any of the big ones without attracting too much attention. That's why I had to get in touch with someone who'd know their real value, and perhaps be able to sell them properly up north.'

At Simon's side, the woman turned abruptly, her overplucked eyebrows drawn together.

'Is he a buyer of pearls?' she asked. 'Is that why he is here? You did not tell me, Ned.'

'I know.' The man smiled awkwardly. 'I told you I was sending for someone who would help us to buy some real diving equipment, so we could really bring up those oysters after I taught you to use it. I was afraid of getting your hopes too high. But actually, that's just what he might do.'

'If the pearls are not worth so much, you will use the money to buy diving equipment to look for more?'

'That's right.'

'But if they're worth enough,' said the Saint, 'you want to pay back eleven thousand dollars to various people, and see if something can be done about your eyes?'

'Yes.'

'And then come back to Consuelo,' said the Saint softly.

'Oh, no,' Ned Yarn said. 'I wouldn't leave here unless she came with me.'

Consuelo stood up with a sudden rough movement that shook the table. She stood beside Yarn with a hand on his shoulder, and his hand went up at once to cover hers.

'I do not like it,' she said. 'How do you know you can trust him?'

'I'll have to risk it,' Yarn said grimly. 'Show him the pearls, Consuelo.'

She stared at the Saint defensively, her eyes hot and hostile and shifting like the eyes of a cornered animal.

'I will not.'

'Consuelo!'

'I cannot,' she said. 'I have already sold them.'

'*What?*'

'*Si, si,*' she said quickly. 'I sold them. To a dealer I met at the Cantina. I was going to surprise you. He gave me five hundred dollars—'

'Five hundred dollars!'

'For a start. He will bring me the rest soon. I have it here.' She twisted away towards the bed and rummaged under the mattress. In a moment she was back, thrusting crumpled bills into his hands. 'There! Count them. It is all there. And there will be more!'

Ned Yarn did not count the bills. He did not even hold them. They spilled over his lap and fluttered down to the floor. He had caught one of Consuelo's wrists, and clung to it with both hands, and his blind face turned up towards her strickenly.

'What is this?' he said in a terrible hoarse voice. 'I never thought you lied to me. But you're lying now. Your voice tells me.'

'I do not lie!'

'Templar,' said Yarn, with a straining throat, 'please help me. There's a pottery jar on the top shelf, in the corner over the stove. Look in it and tell me what you find.'

Simon got to his feet, a little uncertainly. Then he crossed to the corner in three quick strides. There was only one jar that fitted the description. With his height, he could just reach it.

Consuelo writhed and twisted in Yarn's grip like a lassoed wildcat, so that the chair he sat in rocked; and pounded on his head and shoulders with her free fist.

'No, no!' she screamed.

But the blind man's grip held her like an anchor, and she fell still at last as the Saint tilted the jar over one cupped hand, so that the ripple of things rolling from it could be heard over the heavy breathing which was the only other thing that broke the silence.

Simon Templar looked at the dozen or so cheap beads of various sizes brought together in the hollow of his palm, and looked up from them to the defiant streaming eyes of Ned Yarn's woman.

'I think these are the most beautiful pearls I ever saw,' he said.

5

The woman slid down to the floor beside Yarn and sat there with her face pressed against his thigh.

'Why did you lie, Consuelo?' Yarn asked puzzledly. 'What on earth upset you like that?'

'I think I can guess,' said the Saint. 'She was just trying to protect you. After all, neither of you knows me from Adam, and you are taking rather a lot on trust. Probably she wanted time to talk it over with you first.'

The woman sobbed.

Ned Yarn caressed her stringy hair, murmuring little soothing sounds as she clung to his legs.

'It's all right, *querida*.' His face was still troubled. 'But the money – the five hundred dollars. Where did that come from?'

'I bet I can answer that too,' said the Saint. 'She'd held out two or three more small pearls and sold them, and she was saving the money for a surprise present of some kind. Is that right, Consuelo?'

She lifted her head and looked at the Saint.

'No,' she said. 'It is my own money. I earned it and saved it myself. I kept it from you, Ned. I did not want to spend quite all our money on the search for pearls. I thought, perhaps we will never find any pearls, but I would keep saving, and one day perhaps I could take you myself to see if you could be cured. That is the truth.'

Yarn lifted her up and kissed her.

'How blind can a man be?' he said huskily.

'Some people would give their eyes for what you've got,' Simon said.

'And I wish I had mine most so that I could see it. I know how beautiful she must be, but I would like to see her. She is beautiful, isn't she?'

'She is beautiful, Ned.'

'Please, you must both forgive me,' Consuelo said in a low voice. 'Let us have some tequila.'

Simon looked down at the little heap of beads in his hand.

'What do you want me to do with the pearls?' he asked.

The blind man's dark glasses held his gaze like hypnotic hungry eyes.

'Are they really valuable?'

'I'd say they were, but I'm not an expert,' Simon replied, improvising with infinite care. 'They'd have to be sold in the right place, of course. As you may know, individual pearls don't mean so much, unless they're really gigantic. Most pearls are made into necklaces and things like that, which means that they have to be matched, and they gain in value by being put together. And then it's a funny market these days, on account of all the cultured pearls that only an expert can tell from real ones. There are still people who'll spend a fortune on the genuine article, but you don't find them waiting on every jeweller's doorstep. It takes work, and preparation, and patience – and time.'

'But – eventually – they should be worth a lot?'

'Eventually,' said the Saint soberly, 'they may mean more to you than you'd believe right now.'

Ned Yarn's breath came and went in a long sigh.

'That's all I wanted to know,' he said. 'I can wait some more. I guess I'm used to waiting.'

'Do you want me to take the pearls back to the States and see what I can do with them?'

'Yes. And Consuelo and I will go on fishing for more. At least we'll know we aren't wasting our time. Where's that drink you were talking about, Consuelo?' She put the glass in his hand, and he raised it. 'Here's luck to all of us.'

'Especially to you two.' Simon looked at the woman over his glass and said: '*Salud!*'

He wrapped the beads carefully in a scrap of newspaper and tucked it into his pocket.

'Do you mind if Consuelo guides me back from here?' he asked. 'I don't want to get lost.'

'Of course, we don't want that. And thank you for coming.'

The night was the same, perhaps a little cooler, perhaps a little more muted in its secret sounds. The woman's heels tapped the same monotonous rhythm, perhaps a little slower. They walked quite a long way without speaking, as they had before; but now they kept silence as if to make sure that they were beyond the most fantastic range of a blind man's hearing before they spoke.

Simon Templar was glad that the silence lasted as long as it did. He had a lot to think about, to weigh and balance and to look ahead from.

Finally she said, almost timidly, 'I think you understand, *señor*.'

'I think so,' he said; but he waited to hear more from her.

'When he began to be discontented, we went out in the boat and began looking for pearls. For a long time that made him happy. But presently, when we found nothing, he was unhappy again. At last we found some oysters. Then again he had hope. But there were no pearls. So presently, after some more time, he was sad again. It hurt too much to see him despair. So at last I let him find some pearls. At first they were real, I think. I took them from some earrings that my mother gave me. And after that, they were beads.'

'And when you said you sold them—'

'I did sell the real ones, for a few pesos. The rest was money I had saved for him, like the five hundred dollars.'

'Did you mean what I heard you say – that if you could save enough, you meant to take him to a specialist some-where who might be able to bring back his sight?'

There was a long pause before she answered.

'I would have done it when I had the courage,' she said. 'I will do it one day, when I am strong enough. But it will not be easy. Because I know that when he sees me with his eyes, he will not love me any more.'

He felt it all the way through him down to his toes, like the subsonic tremor of an earthquake, the tingling realization of what those few simple words meant.

She was not blind, and she used mirrors. If she had ever deluded herself, it had not been for long. She knew very well what they told her. Homely and aged and scarred as she was, no man such as she had dreamed of as a young girl would ever love her as a young girl dreams of love. Unless he was blind. Even before the ageing had taken hold she had discov-ered that, and seen the infinite emptiness ahead. But one night, some miracle had brought her a blind man . . .

She had taken him in and cared for him in his sickness, find-ing him clean and grateful, and lavished on him all the frus-trated richness of her heart. And out of his helplessness, and for her kindness and the tender beauty of her voice, he had loved her in return. She had used what money she could earn in any way to humour his obsession, to bring him back from despair, to encourage hope and keep alive his dream. And one day she believed she might be able to make at least part of the hope come true, and have him made whole – and let him go.

Simon walked slowly through a night that no longer seemed dark and sordid.

'When he knows what you have done,' he said, 'he should think you the most beautiful woman in the world.'

'He will not love me,' she said without bitterness. 'I know men.'

'Now I can tell you something. He has been blind for nearly ten years. There will have been too many degenerative changes in his eyes by this time. There is hardly any chance at all that an operation could cure him now. And I never thought I could say any man was lucky to be blind, but I think Ned Yarn is that man.'

'Nevertheless, I shall have to try one day.'

'It will be a long time still before you have enough money.'

She looked up at him.

'But the beads you took away. You told him they were worth much. What shall I tell him now?'

It was all clear to Simon now, the strangest crime that he had to put on his bizarre record.

'He will never hear another word from me. I shall just disappear. And presently it will be clear to him that I was a crook after all, as he believes you suspected from the start; and I stole them.'

'But the shock – what will it do to him.'

'He will get over it. He cannot blame you. He will think that your instinct was right all along, and he should have listened to you. You can help him to see that, without nagging him.'

'Then he will want to start looking for pearls again.'

'And you will find them. From time to time I will send you a few for you to put in the oysters. Real ones. You can make them last. You need not find them too often, to keep him hoping. And when you sell them, which you can do as a Mexican without getting in any trouble, you must do what your heart tells you with the money. I think you will be happy,' said the Saint.

6

Mrs Ormond, formerly Mrs Yarn, lay back in her chair and laughed, deeply and vibrantly in her exquisitely rounded throat, so that the ice cubes clinked in the tall glass she held.

'So the dope finally found his level,' she gurgled. 'Living in some smelly slum hovel with a frowzy native slut. While she's whoring in a crummy saloon and dredging up pearl beads to kid him he's something better than a pimp. I might have known it!'

She looked more unreally beautiful than ever in the dim light of the balcony, a sort of cross between a calendar picture and a lecherous trash-writer's imagining, in the diaphanous negligé that she had inevitably put on to await the Saint's return in. Her provocative breasts quivered visibly under the filmy nylon and crowded into its deep-slashed neckline as she laughed and some of the beads rolled out of the unfolded paper in her lap and pattered on the bare floor.

Simon had told her only the skeletal facts, omitting the amplifications and additions which were his own, and waited for her reaction; and this was it.

'I hadn't realized it was quite so funny,' he said stonily.

'You couldn't,' she choked. 'My dear man, you don't know the half of it. Here I come dragging myself down to this ghastly dump, just in case Yarn has really got on to something I couldn't afford to miss; and all he's got is a mulatto concubine and a few beads. And all the time, right here in my jewel case, I've got a string of pearls that were good enough for Catherine of Russia!'

Simon stood very still.

'You have?' he said.

'Just one of those baubles that Ormond used to pass out when he was indulging his sultan complex. Like I told you. I think he only paid about fifteen grand for them at an auction. And me wasting all this time and effort, not to mention yours, on Ned Yarn's imaginary oyster bed!'

At last the Saint began to laugh too, very quietly.

'It is rather delirious,' he said. 'Let me fix you another drink, and let's go on with some unfinished business.'

THE REVOLUTION RACKET

I

'In my time, I've had all kinds of receptions from the police,' Simon Templar remarked. 'Sometimes they want to give me a personal escort out of town. Sometimes they see me as a Heaven-sent fall guy for the latest big crime that they haven't been able to pin on anybody else. Sometimes they just rumble hideous warnings of what they'll do to me if I get out of line while I'm in their bailiwick. But your approach is certainly out of the ordinary.'

'I try not to be an ordinary policeman,' said Captain Carlos Xavier.

They sat in the Restaurant Larue, which has become almost as hardworked and undefinitive a name as Ritz among ambitious food purveyors; this one was in Mexico City, but it made a courageous attempt to live up to the glamorous cosmopolitan connotations of its patronymic. There was nothing traditionally Mexican about its décor, which was rather shinily international, and the menu strove to achieve the same expensive neutrality. However, at Xavier's suggestion, they were eating *pescados blancos*, the delicate little fish of Lake Pátzcuaro which are not quite like anything else in the world, washed down with a bottle of Chilean Riesling; and this, it had already been established, was at the sole invitation and expense of Captain Carlos Xavier.

'Sometimes,' Simon suggested cautiously, 'I've actually been asked to help the police with a problem. But the build-up has never been as lavish as this.'

'I have nothing to ask, except the pleasure of your company,' said Captain Xavier.

He was a large fleshy man with a balding head and a compensatingly luxuriant moustache. He ate with gusto and talked with gestures. His small black eyes were humorous and very bright, but even to Simon's critical scrutiny they seemed to beam honestly.

'All my life I must have been reading about you,' Xavier said. 'Or perhaps I should say, about a person called the Saint. But your identity is no secret now, is it?'

'Hardly.'

'And for almost as long, I have hoped that one day I might have the chance to meet you. I am what I suppose you would call a fan.'

'Coming from a policeman,' said the Saint, 'I guess that tops everything.'

Xavier shook his head vigorously.

'In most countries, perhaps. But not in Mexico.'

'Why?'

'This country was created by revolutions. Many of the men who founded it, our heroes, began as little more than bandits. To this very day, the party in power officially calls itself the Revolutionary Party. So, I think, we Mexicans will always have a not-so-secret sympathy in our hearts for the outlaw – what you call the Robin Hood. For although they say you have broken many laws, you have always been the righter of wrongs – is that not true?'

'More or less, I suppose.'

'And now that I see you,' Xavier went on enthusiastically, and with a total lack of self-consciousness, 'I am even happier. I know that what a man looks like often tells nothing of what he really is. But you are exactly as I had pictured you – tall and strong and handsome, and with the air of a pirate! It is wonderful just to be looking at you!'

The Saint modestly averted his eyes.

This was especially easy to do because the shift permitted him to gaze again at a woman who sat alone at a table across the room. He had noticed her as soon as she entered, and had been glancing at her as often as he could without seeming too inattentive to his host.

With her fair colouring and the unobtrusive elegance of her clothes, she was obviously an American. She was still stretching out her first cocktail, and referring occasionally to the plain gold watch on her wrist: she was, of course, waiting for somebody. The wedding ring on her left hand suggested that it was probably a husband – no lover worthy of her time would be likely to keep such a delectable dish waiting. But, there was no harm in considering, married women did travel alone, and sometimes wait for female friends; they also came to Mexico to divorce husbands; and, as a matter of final realism, an attractive woman wearing a wedding ring abroad was not necessarily even married at all, but might wear it just as a kind of flimsy chastity belt, in the hope of discouraging a certain percentage of unwanted Casanovas. The chances were tenuous enough, but an incorrigible optimist like the Saint could always dream . . .

'And now,' Xavier was saying, 'tell me what you are going to do in Mexico.'

Simon brought his eyes and his ideas back reluctantly.

'I'm just a tourist.' He had said it so often, in so many places, that it was getting to be like a recitation. 'I'm not planning to make any trouble, or get into any. I want to see that new sensation, El Loco, fight bulls. And I'll probably go to Cuernavaca, and Oaxaca, and try the fishing at Acapulco. Just like all the other *gringos*.'

'That is almost disappointing.'

'It ought to make you happy.'

'It is not very exciting, being a policeman here. I should

have enjoyed matching wits with you. Of course, in the end I should catch you, but for a time it would be interesting.'

'Of course,' Simon agreed politely.

'It would have been a great privilege to observe you in action,' Xavier said. 'I have always been an admirer of your methods. Besides, before I caught you, you might even have done some good.'

The Saint raised his eyebrows.

'With anyone so efficient as you on the job, there can't be much left to do.'

'I do my best. But unfortunately, when I make an arrest, I have not always accomplished much.'

'You mean – the court doesn't always take it from there?'

'Much too often.'

'Your candour keeps taking my breath away.'

Xavier shrugged.

'It is the truth. It is not exactly a rare complaint, even in your country. And absolute justice is a much younger idea here. We are still inclined to accept graft as the prerogative of those in power – perhaps it is the legacy of our bandit tradition. It will change, some day. But at the present, there are many times when I would personally like to see a man like you taking the law into your own hands. You will have coffee? And brandy?'

He snapped his fingers at a waiter and gave the order; and the Saint lighted a cigarette and stole another glance at the honey-blonde young woman across the room. She was still alone, and looking a good deal more impatient. It would not be much longer before the moment would be most propitious for venturing a move – if he had only been alone himself. The thought made an irksome subtraction from his full enjoyment of the fact that a police officer was not only buying his dinner but seemed to be handing him an open invitation to resume his career of outlawry.

With a slight effort, he turned again to the more uncommon of the two attractions.

'Are you really wishing I'd un-reform myself,' he asked curiously, 'or are you just dissatisfied with the Government? Maybe another revolution would produce a better system.'

'By no means,' Xavier said quickly. Then, as the Saint's blue eyes continued to rest on him levelly, he received their unspoken question, and said: 'No, I do not say that because I am forced to. The change must come with time and education and growing up. I believe that the Government we have today is as good as any other we would get. No, it is better. In fact, it is already too honest for the people who are most anxious to change it. There is only one party which could seriously threaten a revolution today – and who are its sponsors?'

'You mean José Jalisco?'

'A figurehead – an orator who blows hot air wherever the most pesos tell him! I mean the men behind Jalisco.'

'Who are they?'

'The Enriquez brothers. But I do not suppose your newspapers have room for our scandals. For many years they were making millions, at the expense of the Mexican people, out of Government construction contracts. It was our new President who ordered the investigation which exposed them, and who threw out the officials who helped them. Even now, they may face imprisonment, and fines that would ruin them. They are the ones who would like to see a revolution for Jalisco . . . They are sitting opposite you now, at the table next to the young woman you have been staring at for the last hour.'

Simon winced very slightly, and looked carefully past the blonde.

He had noticed the two men before, observing that they also had been watching the girl and obviously discussing her assets and potentialities, but he had not paid them much attention beyond that. As competition for her favour, he figured that they would not have given him too much trouble. They were excessively well groomed and tailored and manicured, with ostentatious jewellery in their neckties and on their fingers, but their pockmarked features had a cruel and wilful cast that would hardly appeal to a nice girl at first sight. Now that Xavier identified them, the family resemblance was evident.

'The bigger one is Manuel,' Xavier said. 'The smaller is Pablo. But one is as bad as the other. To protect their millions, and to make more, they would not care how many suffered.'

Waiters poured coffee and brought brandy, and Simon took advantage of the diversion to study the Enriquez brothers again. This also allowed him to keep track of the trim young blonde. And this time, when he was looking directly at her, he was able to see that she was looking at him, with what seemed to be considerable interest. It was an effort for him to suppress a growing feeling of frustration.

'Do you seriously believe they could start a revolution?' he asked Xavier.

'I know they have talked of it. Jalisco has a large following. He has the gift, which Hitler and Mussolini had, of inflaming mobs. But a mob, today, can do nothing without modern weapons. That is where the Enriquez brothers come in. They have the money to provide them. One day, I think, they will try to do that. They could be plotting it now, while we look at them.'

'For a couple of desperate conspirators,' Simon commented, 'they don't seem very embarrassed to have you watching them.'

Xavier laughed till his moustache quivered and his second chin shook. But when he could speak again, his voice was as discreetly pitched as it had been all along.

'Me? They have no idea who I am. Any more than you would have known, if I had not introduced myself at your hotel. Who knows an insignificant captain of the police? They deal with chiefs – if they can. They are too big to care whether I exist. But I know about them, as I knew about you, because it is my business to know.'

'And yet there isn't a thing you can do.'

'It takes much proof to accuse such important men. And the bigger they are, the harder it is to get. Probably before I ever get it, it is too late. Another civil war will not be good for Mexico. But I cannot stop a flood, like the Dutch boy, with my little finger.' Xavier shrugged heavily. 'That is why I can be sorry the Saint has become so respectable.'

The Saint gazed at him with an assemblage of conflicting reactions that added up to a poker-faced blankness which could hardly have been improved on deliberately. But before Simon could decide which of a dozen possible replies to make, a waiter bustled up to Xavier with a folded slip of paper on a tray.

Xavier opened it, frowned at it, and pursed his lips over it for several seconds.

'This is a tragedy,' he announced at length, and tucked the note into his pocket.

'Has the shooting started already?' Simon inquired.

'Oh, no. Merely a simple robbery. But it is at the house of a politician, so I must give it my personal attention. My lieutenant is downstairs, and I must go with him.'

Xavier stood up, but put out a restraining hand as the Saint started to rise with him.

'No, please stay here. It is only a routine matter, and would not interest you. Take time to finish your brandy. And have another. I will pay the bill as I go out. I insist.' The bright black eyes twinkled. 'And perhaps after all you will be able to meet the young lady. I shall call you at your hotel soon. *Hasta luego!*'

And with an effusive sequence of handshakes that kept time with the somewhat frantic deluge of his parting speech, he was gone.

Simon Templar sat down again, feeling a trifle breathless by contagion, and poured himself another cup of coffee.

Not too hurriedly, he looked at the lonely young blonde again.

He was just in time to see her greeting a shmoe who had to be her husband.

2

Well, that was the way life was, Simon reflected, as he chain-lit another cigarette. You could spend weeks waiting for a little gentle excitement; and then, when things started happening, there were more of them than you could handle.

A police captain, of all people, points out a couple of apparently ideal candidates for free-lance euthanasia, gives you the why and wherefore, and practically invites you to go ahead and take a crack at them – adding the almost irresistible bait that, although he will thoroughly approve of whatever you do, he is also sure that he will be able to pinch you for it afterwards. But you can't really give your all to this sublime proposition, because you are wishing half the time that he would go away so that you could concentrate on an equally inviting but entirely different temptation to adventure.

So finally he does go away, but only after staying just long enough for the other attraction to slip out of reach.

Then you gripe because you've only got one thing left, and you wanted both. Quite forgetting that you started the evening with nothing.

Oh, what the hell, the Saint thought. He could still murder the Enriquez brothers. And maybe he should murder the blonde's husband too.

There was no doubt about their marital status. The man was far too typical a hard-driving Babbitt to be any girl's secret romance. A good husband, perhaps, but too busy to be a Lothario. He was still in his forties, and not unprepossessing, with a square jaw and horn-rimmed glasses and distinguished flecks of grey at his temples; but you could see that he never left business behind, even as he brought a bulging briefcase with him to dinner.

'Whatever kept you so long?' she asked – not anxiously, not pettishly, but with the controlled and privileged edginess of a long-suffering wife.

'My taxi had a little fender scrape, but it had to be with a police car. You never saw so much commotion and red tape. I almost got locked up as a material witness. I'm sorry, dear – it wasn't my fault.'

He turned to the waiter and ordered two Martinis. The Enriquez brothers looked disappointed, but went on watching them with a kind of morbid curiosity.

'Well,' she said graciously, but after a suitable pause, 'what's the news?'

'I'm getting nowhere. I tell you, Doris, I'm about ready to give up and go home.'

'That isn't like you, Sherm.'

'I know when I'm licked. I've always heard there was a trick to doing business with these South American governments. Now I can vouch for it. You've just got to know the right people – and I don't know them. That seems to be the end of it.'

The Saint was not making any effort to eavesdrop, but he didn't have to. The restaurant was quiet, and they were talking in clear normal voices, as if they were confident in the security of speaking a foreign language; but that very contrast made it easier for him to separate their conversation from the background tones of Spanish.

The waiter brought him another snifter of Rémy Martin, with the parting compliments of Captain Xavier, and went on to deliver two Martinis across the room. Simon gazed innocently into space, and let his ears receive what came to them.

'What an incredible hard-luck story it is,' the husband said glumly. 'First I get a contract to supply all those rifles and machine-guns to Iran – over the heads of all the big arms companies. Then I pull all the strings in Washington to get an export permit, which everyone said couldn't be done. Then I manage to charter a boat to carry them, which isn't so easy these days. And then, two days after the boat sails, they have a revolution in Iran and the new government cancels the order!'

'And you've paid for the guns, haven't you? Your money's tied up.'

'It sure is. But I wasn't worried until now. I'd gotten them legally out of the States, so I could still sell them anywhere in the world where I could find a buyer. And I thought Mexico would be a cinch. Their Army equipment is nearly all out of date anyhow. And yet I can't even get to talk to anyone. I've got fifty thousand late-model rifles and five thousand machine-guns cruising around the Caribbean, with five million rounds of ammunition – and nobody seems to want 'em!'

It should be recorded as a major testimonial to Simon Templar's phenomenal self-control that for an appreciable time he did not move a muscle. But he felt as unreal as if he had been sitting still in the midst of an earthquake. It required a conscious adjustment for him to realize that the seismic shock he experienced was purely subjective, that the mutter of other voices around had not changed key or missed a beat, that the ceiling had not fallen in and all the glassware shattered in one cataclysmic crash.

But nothing of the sort had happened. Nothing at all. Of course not.

'It's not your fault, Sherm,' the wife was saying. 'You'll just have to try somewhere else. There are plenty of other countries, and I've always wanted to see them.'

'I don't know what'd make it better anywhere else. I guess I don't know the right way to approach these people.'

It began to dawn on the Saint that his continued immobility could eventually become as conspicuous, to a watchful eye, as if he had jumped out of his skin.

With infinite casualness, he removed a length of ash from his cigarette, and inhaled with heroic moderation.

Then he lifted his brandy glass, and let his eyes wander across the room.

The Enriquez brothers were watching the American couple too, and their expression made him think of a couple of Walt Disney wolves discovering a hole in the fence of a sheep corral.

'For two cents,' said the husband morosely, 'I'd start looking around for someone who wants to organize a revolution here, and offer to sell *him* the guns. It might do me a lot more good.'

Manuel Enriquez spoke earnestly to Pablo, and Pablo nodded vehemently.

Manuel stood up and approached the adjacent table.

'Please excuse me,' he said in good English, 'but I could not help hearing what you were saying.'

The couple exchanged guilty glances, but Manuel smiled reassuringly.

'I appreciate your problem. As you said, it is important to know the right people. I believe my brother and I could help you.'

'Gosh,' said the husband. 'That sounds wonderful! Are you serious?'

'Absolutely. May I introduce myself? I am Manuel Enriquez. That is my brother Pablo.'

'Sherman Inkler,' said the husband, whipping out a wallet and a card from the wallet. 'And of course this is Mrs Inkler.'

'Oh, Sherm!' Doris Inkler gasped. 'This could be the break you've been waiting for!'

'We can soon find out,' Manuel said. 'But this is not a good place to discuss business. You have not yet ordered your dinner. May I invite you to another place where we can talk more privately? My car is outside, and you shall be my guests.'

As the Inklers and Pablo stood up simultaneously, he waved imperiously to the head waiter and shepherded them towards the stairs, pausing only to take both checks and sign them on the way out. It was in that brief stoppage that the blonde turned and looked at the Saint again, so intently that he knew, with utter certainty, that something had clicked in her memory, and that she knew who he was.

3

The implications of that long deliberate look would have sprinkled goose-pimples up his spine – if there had been room for any more. But he had just so much capacity for horripilation, and all of it had already been pre-empted by the scene he had witnessed just previously. The Saint had long ago conditioned himself to accept coincidences unblinkingly that would have staggered anyone who was less accustomed to them: it was much the same as a prize-fighter becoming inured to punishment, except that it was more pleasant. He had come to regard them as no more than the recurrent evidence of his unique and blessed destiny, which had ordained that wherever he turned, whether he sought it or not, he must always collide with adventure. But the supernatural precision and consecutiveness with which everything had unfolded that evening would have been enough to send spooky tingles up a totem pole.

And yet the immediate result was to leave him sitting as impotently apart as the spectator of a play when the first-act curtain comes down. With the departure of the Enriquez brothers and the Inklers, he was as effectively cut off from the action as if it were unrolling in another world. The instinctive impulse, of course, was to follow; but cold reason instantaneously knocked that on the head. Manuel Enriquez had said they would go to a place where they could talk privately, and the Saint felt sure it would be just that. If any of them saw him again in their vicinity, it was a ten-to-one bet that they would have remembered him from the restaurant anyway, and drawn the obvious conclusion. But that last long look from the blonde had taken it out of the realm of risk into the confines of stark certainty.

He tried to analyse that look again in retrospect, to determine what else might have been in it beyond simple recognition, while another department of his mind reached for philosophical consolation for the quirk of circumstance that kept him pinned to his chair.

Why did he have to follow, anyhow? He could predict exactly what would happen next. The Enriquez brothers would offer to buy the shipload of guns. And Sherman Inkler, of course, would have his price . . .

The full significance of the blonde's look eluded him. Each time he tried to reconstruct and reassess it, he was halted before an intangible wall of inscrutability.

He finished his cognac and coffee and stood up at last, and went down the stairs and through the bar out to the Paseo de la Reforma. It was raining, as it can do in Mexico City even in late spring, and the moist air had an exotic aroma of overloaded drains. One day, they say, the whole city will sink back and disappear into the swampy depths of the crater from which it arose. On such nights, as in any other city, there is always a dearth of taxis, but the Saint was fortunate enough to meet one unloading customers for the movie theatre next door.

He had had plans to go prowling in search of distraction later that evening, whenever he got rid of Xavier; but now the drive had evaporated. Opportunity had already knocked as often as it was likely to do in one night.

'Al Hotel Comee,' he said.

The Comee is not the plushest hotel in Mexico City, being a few minutes' drive from the fashionable centre of town; but its entirely relative remoteness makes it quieter than the more publicized caravanserais, and the Saint preferred it for that reason.

He sat on his bed and turned the pages of the telephone directory.

Would Carlos Xavier have an unlisted number? But Xavier was sure to be still tied up with a burgled politico, in any case. And the Saint was far from obsessed with the idea of talking to Xavier again – just yet.

What kind of hotel would the Inklers be staying at? There could only be a limited number of possibilities.

He picked up the telephone.

'The Reforma Hotel, please,' he said.

After the usual routine of sound effects, the connection was made.

'Mr Inkler, please,' he said. 'Mr Sherman Inkler. I-n-k-l-e-r.'

'One moment, please.'

It was longer than that. Then the Reforma operator said: 'I'm sorry, there is no Mr Inkler here.'

'Thank you,' said the Saint.

He lighted a cigarette and stretched himself out more comfortably on the bed while he jiggled the telephone bracket. This method of search might take some time. But it was bound to succeed eventually. When he got the Comee operator back, he said: 'Get me the Del Prado.'

He drew another blank there. But all it would take was patience.

He was starting to recall his own operator again when there was a knock on the door. He hung up with a frown, and stood up and opened it.

Doris Inkler stood outside.

'You don't have to try any longer, unless you particularly want to,' she said. 'May I come in?'

The Saint was not given to exaggerated reactions. He did not fall over backwards in an explosion of sparks and stars like a character in the funny papers, with his eyebrows shooting up through his hair. He may have felt rather like it, but he was able to resist the inclination. In his memoirs, he would probably list it among the finest jobs of resisting he ever did.

He waved his cigarette with an aplomb that had no counterpart in his internal sensations.

'But of course,' he said cordially. 'This proves that telepathy is still better than telephones.'

She stepped in just as calmly, and he closed the door.

'I could have let you work a lot longer, if I'd wanted to make it tough for you,' she said. 'But I got tired of standing outside.'

Her head and eyes made an indicative movement back and upwards, and he followed their direction to the open transom above the door. He shut it.

'You must have a very big kind heart,' he said.

'It's a pretty tedious way to track anyone down,' she said. 'I know. That's how I located you.'

'Did you make a deal or wash out with the Enriquez brothers so quickly?'

'They dropped me off first, and just took Sherman along. I think they have an old-world prejudice against having wives sit in on business conferences. So I was probably able to start calling sooner than you did. Besides, I was lucky.'

'Where, as a matter of interest, are you staying?'

'In Room 611.'

The Saint sighed.

'And this is probably the last hotel I'd have tried. It would have seemed too easy. Whereas you, being a simple-minded woman, probably tried it first.'

'Correct. But let's change that "simple-minded" to "economical". This was the one place I could try before I started to run up a telephone bill.'

He cleared some things from a chair, and she sat down. He gave her a cigarette, lighted it, and sat on the end of the bed. At last he was actually as relaxed and at ease as he had contrived to seem from the beginning. He wondered why he had ever allowed himself to get in a stew about the apparent dead end he had run into. He should have known that such a fantastically pat and promising beginning could not possibly peter out, so long as there was such an obviously plot-conscious genius at work. Inevitably the thread would have been brought back to him even if he had done nothing but sit and wait for it.

But underneath his coolly interested repose he was as wary as if he had been closeted with a coy young tigress. Perhaps everything would remain cosy and kitteny; but he had no illusions about the basic hazards of the situation.

'It's nice to feel that our hearts are so in tune,' he remarked. 'I was determined to find you again, regardless of cost. You were a little thriftier about it, but no less determined. And so we meet. Fate failed to keep us apart, and at this moment is probably gnashing the few teeth it can have left. However, there's still one small point. I had plenty of opportunities to hear your name. But how did you know mine?'

'I recognized you, Mr Templar – as I think you knew.'

'We haven't met before.'

'No.'

'So you've seen my picture and read about me.'

'Right. And now it's time you let me ask a question. Why were you so anxious to find me?'

Simon considered his reply.

'Any mirror would tell you better than I can. But let's say that when I first saw you alone, I was hoping you'd stay that way for long enough for us to get acquainted. I was sort of tied up at the moment, if you remember. Then, when your husband showed up, I could see you were much too good for him. After thinking it over, I decided that he's the dull type that it's almost a public duty to cuckold. I was planning to find out if you agreed.'

Her eyes widened a fraction but did not blink. They were a darker blue than his own, and there were smoky shadows in their depths. Blue is conventionally a cool colour, but he realized that her shade could have the heat potential of a blowtorch flame.

'You don't try very hard to be subtle, do you?' she said, and said it without any indignation.

'Not always. Especially when a gal seems to have similar ideas of her own. You didn't track me down just to ask for my autograph, did you?'

'No. My turn again. What do you know about the Enriquez brothers?'

'That they're big tycoons down here, and tough babies. That they've specialized in robbing the Mexican public through government contracts obtained by graft and corruption. That they were recently investigated and exposed by the present administration, and are temporarily out of business and facing a possible rest period in the hoosegow. That they would therefore like to see a fast change in the regime. That they are backing a fast-changer named José Jalisco, who has the necessary wind to rouse the rabble, and would love to buy some toys that go bang for his followers. That this makes them ideal customers for a homeless shipload of arms and ammunition.'

'You seem to have found out a lot.'

'It was poured into my ear, on what I believe to be excellent authority. Shouldn't that make it my turn next? Why were you looking for me, if it wasn't just to tell me how wonderful you think I am?'

'I wanted to ask how you felt about that gun deal.'

The Saint grinned.

'That's a neat reverse,' he said appreciatively.

'Well?'

She was not smiling. The dusky warmth in her eyes was stilled and held back, perhaps like a force in reserve.

Simon gazed at her directly for several seconds while he made a decision. He stubbed out his cigarette gently in an ashtray.

'I don't like it,' he answered.

'Do you really care whether they have one more revolution here?'

'Yes, I do,' he said. 'It may be rather dreamy and sentimental of me, but I care. If I thought it had a chance of doing some good, I might feel differently. But I know about this one. Its only real objective would be to get a couple of top-flight grafters off the hook and put them back in business. To achieve that, a lot of wretched citizens and stooges would be killed and maimed, and thousands more would be made even more miserable than they are. I wouldn't like that.'

'Not even if it dropped a very nice piece of change into your own lap?'

His mouth hardened.

'Not even if it dropped me the keys to Fort Knox,' he said coldly. 'I can always steal a few million without killing anyone, or making nearly so many people unhappy.'

She flicked her cigarette jerkily. The ash made a grey splash on the carpet.

'So if you could, you'd try to stop Sherman making a deal.'

'I'll go further. I intend to do my God-damnedest to louse it up.'

'I had an idea that was what you'd say.'

'If you'd read anything about me worth reading, you wouldn't even have had to ask.'

She took a slow deep breath. It stirred fascinating contours under the soft silk of her dress.

'That's good,' she said. 'I just had to be sure. Now I know you'll be with us. We don't have any cargo of guns to sell. We're just trying to clean up in the bunko racket, with a bit of that Robin Hood touch you used to specialize in. The whole pitch was just a build-up to take the Enriquez brothers.'

4

Simon Templar stood up, unfolding his length inch by inch. He felt for the packet of cigarettes in his shirt pocket. He drew out a cigarette and placed it between his lips. He stroked his lighter and put it to the cigarette. He exhaled a thin jet of smoke and put the lighter back in his pocket. All his movements were extremely slow and careful, as if he had been balancing on a tightrope over a whirling void. They had to be, while he waited for his fragmented coordinates to settle down, like a spun kaleidoscope, into a new pattern. But by this time his capacity for dizziness was fortunately a little numbed. The human system can only absorb so many jolts in one evening without losing some of its pristine vigour of response.

'I see,' he said. 'I suppose I should have guessed it when your husband came bouncing in and spilled all the beans so loudly and clearly at the very next table to Manuel and Pablo – after you'd kept them watching you long enough to be quite sure they'd be listening.'

'He wasn't meant to wait quite so long,' she said, 'but he did get held up.'

'So there is no ship. And no guns.'

She shook her head.

'There is a ship. It's cruising in the Gulf of Mexico right now. It has a lot of crates on board – full of rocks. There are also two or three on top which do have rifles and machine-guns in them, which can be opened for inspection. We weren't expecting the Enriquez brothers to put out a lot of cash without being pretty convinced about what they were buying.'

'That sounds like quite an investment.'

'It was. But we can afford it. If it works out, we'll pick up at least half a million dollars.'

The Saint rubbed his hands softly together, just once.

'A truly noble swindle,' he murmured with restrained rapture. 'Boldly conceived, ingeniously contrived, unstintingly financed, slickly dramatized, professionally played – and one of the classics of all time for size. I wish I'd thought of it myself.'

For the first time in a long while, a trace of a smile touched her lips.

'You approve?'

'Especially in the choice of pigeons.'

'I'm glad of that. I picked them myself, and planned it all for them. I thought it made quite a Saintly set-up. In fact, I should really give you most of the credit. I was thinking of things I'd read about you, and the way you used to do jobs like this, all the time I was figuring it out.'

He studied her again, for the first time with purely intellectual appraisal.

'It begins to sound as if you were the brains of the Inkler partnership.'

'Sometimes I am. Of course, Sherm wasn't doing so badly when I teamed up with him. But this one was my very own brain-child.'

'And was it all your own idea, too, to come and talk to me just now?'

'We agreed on it. I had a chance to get in a word with him alone, when they dropped me off. I told him I'd recognized you, and who you were. We both knew we'd have to do some fresh figuring, fast. He left it to me. As a matter of fact, he didn't have much choice. The Enriquez brothers were waiting. He said whatever I did was okay with him, but for Christ's sake do something.'

'Well,' said the Saint helpfully, 'what are you going to do?'

She raised her eyes to his face.

'I've told you the whole story. And I'm hoping you're not sore at me for trying to imitate your act.'

'Of course not,' Simon assured her heartily. 'If you mean, for baiting such a beautiful trap to skin a pair of sidewinders like Manuel and Pablo. I wish a lot more people would take up the sport. However . . .' His brows drew together and his gaze slanted at her shrewdly. 'I had my eye on them too, even if you saw them first.'

'And you should get a royalty for being my inspiration.' She put out her cigarette, escaping his steady scrutiny only for a moment, and looked at him again. 'All right. Would you be satisfied if we split three ways?'

He didn't move.

'You, me, and Sherman?' he said.

'Yes. After all, we've spent a lot of money, and done a lot of groundwork.'

Simon walked over to the window and looked out. It seemed to have stopped raining, but the streets below were shiny with water. He gazed over the nearer rooftops and the scattered lights to the hazy glow of illumination that hung over the city's centre. He had seldom felt that life was so rich and bountiful.

There may well be among the varied devotees of these chronicles some favoured individual who has once experienced a certain feeling of elation upon learning that a hitherto undreamed-of uncle has gone to join the heavenly choir, leaving him a half-dozen assorted oil wells. Such a one might have a faint conception of the incandescent beatitude that was welling up in the Saint's ecstatic soul. A very faint and protopathic conception. For the fundamentally dreary mechanics of inheriting a few mere fountains of liquid lucre cannot really be compared with the blissful largesse that the Saint saw Providence decanting on him from its upturned cornucopia. This had poetry; this fell into the kind of artistic pattern that made music in his heart.

He turned at last.

'Will you just mail me my share,' he asked, 'or am I expected to help?'

'Is the deal okay?'

'You must remind me some day to warn you about being too generous, in this racket.'

She let out breath in an almost inaudible sigh, sinking a little deeper in the chair. It was the first proof she had given that she had been under tension before.

'You could help a lot.'

'Tell me.'

'Frankly,' she said, 'the only thing I've been worried about is the payoff. First, they'll want to be sure that we've really got the guns. That's taken care of. They can take a motor-boat and go out a few miles from Vera Cruz or Tampico, and meet our boat. All right. Then we'll come to the question of delivery. That cargo can't be unloaded at a regular port. So I expect them to pick some quiet spot along the coast where it can be brought in at dead of night.'

'How do you manage to be so beautiful and have this kind of brain?' he asked admiringly.

'I'm only thinking it out the way you would.' There was nothing coy about her now: it was all business. 'So we agree to do that. But we can't count on them giving us the money and trusting that we'll deliver. Most probably, they'll want to pay off at the landing place, when the cargo starts coming ashore. We'd have to agree to that too. And then suppose they decided to double-cross us – to take the cargo and keep their money?'

'They'd be afraid of you tipping off the cops . . . But of course, if they were going that far, they could shut you up permanently.'

'And Sherman isn't the fighting type. Even if he had a gun, he wouldn't know how to use it.'

'How about your crew on the boat?'

'They're only half in on the caper. We told them we were only trying to run in a batch of illegal slot machines, and hired them for a flat price. You can imagine what a cut they'd have wanted if we'd said anything about guns. They don't think they're taking much of a risk, and I'd hate to rely on them in a real jam.'

'But you're paying them out of your share?'

'Call it part of the investment I mentioned. That's why I couldn't offer you better than a three-way split. When you work it out, you'll really be getting closer to half of the net.'

He nodded.

'I'm afraid my lecture on the folly of being too generous isn't going to do you much good when I get around to it, Doris.' The twist of his mouth was humorously speculative. 'However, since you made the terms, I guess a little body-guarding isn't too much help to ask in return for a cut like that.'

She stood up from the chair and moved towards him. She kept on coming towards him, slowly, until the tips of her breasts touched his chest.

'If that isn't enough,' she said, 'there might be a personal bonus . . . Sherman won't be back for a long while yet. You've got time to think it over.'

5

Doris Inkler phoned him at nine o'clock, as he was stepping out of the shower, and asked him to join them in their suite for breakfast. A few minutes later he knocked on the door, and she opened it. She looked fresh and cool in a light cotton print, and her eyes were only warm and intimate for an instant, before she turned to introduce him to her husband.

'Doris has told me the deal,' Inkler said, shaking hands in the brisk business-like way which was so much a part of his act that it must have become a part of himself. 'This caper is all her baby, so it's okay with me. Glad to have you on our side.'

He looked a little tired and nervous.

'I didn't get in till three this morning,' he explained. 'These Mexicans don't seem to care about bedtime. I guess they make up for it with their siestas. However, everything's set.'

A waiter wheeled in a table set with three places.

'We ordered bacon and eggs for you,' Inkler said. 'Hope that's all right.'

'I'm starved,' Doris said. 'While you were dining and wining with the brothers, you'd politely got rid of me.'

'I thought you'd get yourself something here,' Inkler said.

'I was too busy locating Mr Templar. And after that – too busy.'

She was pouring coffee as she said it, and she didn't look at Simon.

'I'm sorry,' said the Saint. 'I forgot all about that. I was too interested myself.'

The waiter was gone, and they ate.

'The Enriquez boys are calling for us at half past eleven,' Inkler said. 'By that time they'll have arranged for the cash. They'll drive us to Vera Cruz. They've got a fishing boat there, and we'll go out and look at the cargo. I sent a radio-telegram to our captain last night, telling him to meet us twenty miles out. I just hope it isn't too rough.'

'How are you going to account for me?' Simon asked.

'That's easy,' Doris said. 'You're Sherman's partner, just arrived from the States. You were worried about him making no progress, and flew down unexpectedly to see whether you could help.'

'Your faith in me is almost embarrassing. How did you know I'd have the equipment to disguise myself, in case one of the brothers happened to remember seeing me at another table last night?'

'If you hadn't, we could have lent it to you. But I couldn't imagine the Saint being without it. I expect you have another name with you, too.'

'Tombs,' said the Saint. 'Sebastian Tombs.'

He still had a sentimental attachment to the absurd alias that he had used so often, but he felt reasonably confident that the Enriquez brothers would not have heard of it.

'Have you got a gun?' Inkler asked.

Simon patted his left side, under the arm.

'I can take care of Manuel and Pablo, and maybe some of their friends, if they try any funny business,' he said. 'But whether I can take care of the whole Mexican *gendarmerie* is another matter. Even if everything goes according to plan, it may not be long before they find out that your packing cases aren't all full of artillery. Then they might have the cops look-ing for us on some phony charge – as well as Jalisco's bully boys. I don't think Mexico will be the ideal vacation spot for us after this. What were your plans for after you got the dough?'

Inkler looked at his wife, leaving her to answer.

'I've found out that there's a night plane from here to Havana that stops at Vera Cruz at two o'clock in the morning,' she said. 'It should be just right for us. I'll make the reservations while you're getting disguised, if that suits you.'

The Saint seldom used an elaborate disguise, and in this case he did not have to conceal his identity from anyone who knew him but only from two men who might possibly have recalled him from having casually noticed him the night before. With plenty of grey combed into his dark hair, and the addition of a neat grey moustache and tinted glasses, he was sure that the Enriquez brothers would see nothing familiar about him. Even the Inklers, when he first met them again, looked at him blankly.

The Enriquez brothers arrived with un-Mexican punctuality. Simon was introduced to them in the lobby, and they accepted Inkler's explanation of his presence with no signs of suspicion.

Outside, they had two matching light yellow Cadillacs. Chauffeurs opened the doors simultaneously as they came out. Manuel Enriquez ushered them into one of the cars; and Simon, always considerate of his own comfort on a long trip, quietly slipped into the front seat. Manuel followed the Inklers into the back. Pablo waved to them and turned away.

'He goes in the other car,' Manuel explained. 'He has the money.'

He said it with a smile, almost passing it off as a joke, so that the implication was inoffensive. But it left no doubt, if there had ever been any, that the Enriquez brothers were not babes in the woods. Nor, Simon believed, were their chauffeurs. The one beside him, whom he was able to study at more length, had the shoulders of a prizefighter and a face that had not led a sheltered life.

On the other hand, these evidences of sensible caution did

not necessarily mean that there was a doublecross in prospect, and the Saint saw no reason why he should not let himself at least enjoy the trip. Manuel was a good host in his way, even if he made Simon think of a hospitable alligator, pointing out the landmarks along the way and making agreeable small talk about Mexican customs and conditions, without any reference to politics. Nor was there any mention of the object of their journey – but, after all, there was no more at that moment to discuss.

They had lunch at Puebla, and then rolled on down the long serpentine road to the coast. After a while the Saint went to sleep.

It was early evening when they reached Vera Cruz, and drove through the hot noisy streets out to the comparative tranquillity of the Mocambo.

'We will stay here tonight,' Manuel said. 'While they take in our bags we will get something to eat. It may be late before we can have dinner.'

After sandwiches and cold beer they got into Manuel's car again. A short drive took them to the Club Nautico. As they got out, Simon observed that Pablo's twin Cadillac was no longer behind them.

'If all is well, we shall meet him presently,' Manuel said.

He guided them to the dock where a shiny new Chris-Craft with fishing chairs and outriggers was tied up. The crew of two who helped them aboard were identical in type with the chauffeurs, and no less efficiently taciturn. The lines were cast off at once, and the big engines came to life, one after the other, with deep hollow roars. The boat idled out into the darkening harbour.

'Tell us where we are to go,' Manuel said.

'North-east,' Inkler said, 'and twenty miles out.'

Enriquez translated to the captain at the wheel.

'Let us go inside and be comfortable,' he said. 'I have

whisky, gin and tequila. In an hour we should be able to see your boat.'

The time did not pass too badly, although Simon would have preferred to stay on deck. It was noisy in the cabin, with the steady drone of the engines and the rush of water, so that a certain effort had to be made to talk and to listen. But fortunately for their comfort there was very little sea, and the speeding boat did not bounce much.

He was checking his watch for the exact end of the estimated hour when the engines reduced their volume of sound suddenly and the boat sagged down and surged heavily as its own wave overtook it. They all went out with unanimous accord into the after-cockpit, and Simon saw the lights and silhouette of a ship ahead of them. A moment later, Enriquez switched on a spotlight and sent its beam sweeping over the other vessel. It was a squat and very dilapidated little coastal freighter of scarcely three hundred tons which would certainly have looked like having a rough voyage to Iran, if anybody but the Saint had been critical of such details at that moment. An answering light blinked from her bridge, three times.

'That's it,' Inkler said.

'What you call, on the nose?' Enriquez said with solid satisfaction.

As the Chris-Craft drew alongside, the freighter lowered a boarding ladder. Doris Inkler stood beside the Saint.

'We'll wait for you here,' she said.

They watched Inkler and Enriquez clamber up over the side and disappear. Simon lighted two cigarettes and gave her one. She stayed close to him, watching the Mexican captain and mate as they made a rope fast to the ladder and hung fenders over the rubbing strake.

'This is the first place we could have trouble,' she said in a low voice. 'If Manuel wants one of the wrong cases opened . . .'

'Don't worry until it happens,' he said.

But he could feel her tenseness, and he was a little tense himself for what seemed like an interminable time, but by his watch was less than a half-hour, until at last Inkler and Enriquez came down the ladder again and joined them in the smaller boat's cockpit. Then he could tell by the subtly different confidence of both men that there had been no trouble.

Manuel spoke briefly to the captain, who yelled at the mate, and the bow line was cast off. Water widened between the two hulls, and the Chris-Craft engines grumbled again. Manuel shepherded the Inklers and the Saint below.

He poured four drinks in four clean glasses, and raised one of them.

'To our good fortunes,' he said.

'Is everything all right?' Doris asked, holding on to her glass.

'Your husband is a good businessman. He has the right things for the right customers.'

Only the most captious analyst might have thought she was a fraction slow with her response.

'Oh, Sherman!'

She flung her arms around Inkler's neck and kissed him joyously. Then she turned to the Saint and did the same to him. Inkler watched this with a steady smile.

'Your boat is now following us to a little fishing village, where I have men waiting to unload the cargo,' Manuel said.

'Is it far?'

'We have to go slower, of course. But it will not be too long. About three hours. And we have plenty to drink.'

'Pablo Enriquez is waiting there with the money,' Inkler said to the Saint.

Simon remembered that he had the privileged role of a partner.

'Exactly when is it to be paid?' he inquired. 'I hope Mr

Enriquez won't be offended, but business is business. He wanted to see what we had to offer before he committed himself, and quite rightly. Now I don't think we should have to unload all that stuff until it's paid for.'

Manuel grinned like a genial saurian.

'As soon as I tell Pablo it's okay, he gives you the money. Five hundred thousand American dollars. In cash!'

There was nothing more to be said; but the rest of the voyage seemed to take far more than three times as long as the trip out. The Chris-Craft wallowed along sluggishly, rolling a little with the swell; they all realized that her speed had to be cut down to let the freighter keep up with her, but still their nerves chafed against the restraint, aching impatiently and impossibly for the throttles to open and the exhaust to belch in booming crescendo and the ship to lighten and lift up and skim with all the throbbing speed of which she was capable, lancing through the time between them and the climax ahead. That was how Simon felt, and he knew that two others felt exactly as he did and worse.

There was plenty to drink, as Manuel said, but they could not even take advantage of that to deaden the consciousness of crawling minutes. Sipping lightly and at a studiously sober pace himself, Simon noted that the Inklers were doing the same. Once Sherman emptied his glass rather hurriedly, and earned an unmistakable cold stare from his wife; after that he left the refill untouched for a long time. Only Enriquez was under no inhibition, but the alcohol seemed to have no effect on him, unless it was to confirm his hard-lipped good humour.

'Perhaps one day we do some more business, but in the open,' was the closest he came to referring to the lawless purpose of their association. 'It is like Prohibition in your country, is it not? When the law changes, the bootleggers become importers. But until then, it is better you forget all about tonight.'

Watching him with ruthless detachment, the Saint was unable to detect any foreshadowing of a double-cross. And, after all, it was entirely possible that the Enriquez brothers would be prepared to pay for what they thought they were getting, and even consider it cheap at the price. At the infinite end of three hours, he was almost convinced that Manuel was prepared to complete his infamous bargain. Yet he could not relax.

At last, after three eternities, there was a change of volume in the purr of the engines, and the boat seemed to be rolling less, and muffled voices shouted on deck. Manuel put down his glass and went out quickly, and they followed.

The night air was still warm and humid, but it was refreshing after the stuffy cabin. The sky overhead was an awning of rich velvet sprinkled with unrealistically brilliant stars, and on both sides Simon saw the black profiles of land sharply cut out against it; over the bow, at the end of the bay, he saw the scattered yellow window lights of a small village, and closer than that there were other lights down by the water, flashlights that moved and danced. Searching around for the ugly shape of the little freighter, he found it looming so close astern that it was momentarily alarming, until he realized that it was hardly moving. The Mexican captain was yelling up at it and waving his arms. Enriquez took over, translating: 'Stop here! You can't go any farther!'

The anchor came down from the freighter with a clanking of chain and a splash. Enriquez turned to Inkler.

'We can go in to the dock, but he is too big. My men will come out in smaller boats to unload.'

Inkler relayed the information, shouting upwards at the freighter's bridge. He added, 'Don't let 'em have the stuff till I give the signal!'

A voice shouted back, unnautically, 'Okey-doke.'

The Mexican captain shoved the clutches forward, and the Chris-Craft purred away.

In a few minutes they were alongside the ramshackle dock where the flashlights bobbed. There were at least a dozen men on it, and a slight aroma of fish and sweat and garlic; the silent shadowy figures gave an impression of roughness and toughness, but only an occasional glimpse of detail could be seen when a light moved. Manuel stepped ashore first, and the Saint followed him and gave his hand to Doris Inkler to help her. Her hand was cold, and kept hold of his even after she had joined him on the rickety timbers. Sherman Inkler stumbled on to the pier after them.

Enriquez seemed to sense the defensiveness of their grouping for he said reassuringly, 'They are all friends of our friend Jalisco. Don't worry. This village is one of ours.'

He guided them through the opening ranks and off the dock. It felt good to the Saint to stretch his legs again on solid ground. The dim square outlines of several parked trucks loomed around them; then another man alone, whose face was faintly spotlighted in the darkness by the glow of a cigar. It was Pablo.

The two brothers talked quickly and briefly in Spanish, and Manuel said mostly '*Si, si,*' and '*Está bien.*'

'This way,' Pablo said.

He led them a little distance from the trucks, to where one of the yellow Cadillacs was parked under a tree, with one of the burly chauffeurs beside it. He went around to the back and unlocked the boot. An automatic light went on as it opened, illuminating one medium-sized suitcase inside.

'That is for you,' Pablo said.

Inkler stepped slowly forward. He opened the suitcase gingerly, as if expecting it to be booby-trapped. Simon felt Doris tremble a little at his shoulder. Then they saw the neat bundles of green bills that filled the case.

'You may count it,' Manuel said.

Inkler took out one of the packages of currency and

thumbed through it methodically. He compared it with the others for thickness. Doris joined him and began to count packages, rummaging to the very bottom of the case. Sherman pulled out occasional bills and examined them very closely under the light. Most of them were twenties and fifties.

Simon Templar watched from where he stood, and also let his eyes travel all around and turned his head casually to look behind him. His muscles and reflexes were poised on a hair trigger. But he could neither see nor hear any hint of a closing ambush. The husky chauffeur stood a little apart, like a statue. The Enriquez brothers talked together in low tones, and the only scraps of their conversation that the Saint could catch were concerned entirely with their arrangements for storing and distributing the ordance that they thought they were buying.

'I'm satisfied,' Sherman Inkler said at last.

Manuel lighted a cigar.

'Good. Then you will give the signal to your boat?'

'Of course.'

Manuel led him back into the gloom, in the direction of the pier.

Doris Inkler closed and fastened the suitcase and pulled it out of the car boot. She unbalanced a little as the full weight came on her arm, and put it down on the ground.

'It's heavy,' she said with a nervous laugh; and as the Saint stepped up to feel it, out of curiosity, she said: 'Give me a cigarette.'

He gave her one, and Pablo lighted it.

'It is a lot of money,' Pablo said. 'It will buy many pretty things, if you have an appreciative husband.'

'I'll feel safer with it when it's turned into traveller's cheques,' said the Saint.

Pablo laughed.

They made forced and trivial conversation until Simon heard Manuel and Sherman returning.

Now, if there was to be any treachery on the part of the Enriquez brothers, it would have to show itself. The Saint's weight was on the balls of his feet, his right hand ready to move like a striking snake; but still the movement that he was alert for did not come.

'I am afraid it will take several hours to unload everything,' Manuel said. 'Would you like to go back on the boat and have some more drinks?'

Doris looked at her husband.

'Can't we go back to the hotel? I'm tired, and famished – and I think some mosquitoes are eating me.'

'Pablo and I must stay here,' Manuel said. 'And we need all our men. Even the chauffeur should be helping. However . . . Would you like to take the car? One of you can drive. It is an easy road to Vera Cruz. You cannot get lost.'

He gave directions.

'But what about you?' Inkler protested half-heartedly.

'We will come later, on one of the trucks. Do not wait up for us.'

Almost incredulously, they found themselves getting into the Cadillac. Sherman picked up the suitcase full of money and put it in the front seat, and got in beside it, behind the wheel. 'Don't want to let it out of my sight,' he said with an empty grin. Manuel and Pablo kissed the hand of Doris, and she got in the back seat. Simon shook hands with them and got in after her. In a mere matter of seconds they were on their way.

They must have driven more than a mile in unbelieving silence. It was as if they were afraid that even there the Enriquez brothers might overhear them, or that a careless word might shatter a fragile spell . . .

And then suddenly, uncontrollably, Doris electrified the stillness with a wild banshee shriek.

'We did it!' she screamed. 'We've got the money, and we're off. *We did it!*'

She leaned forward and grasped her husband's shoulders and shook them.

'Better than I ever hoped for,' Sherman said shakily. 'I thought at the very least we'd have a chauffeur to get rid of. But we're on our own already. Now pull yourself together!'

Doris fell back, giggling hysterically.

The Saint's right hand slid unobtrusively under his coat, fingered the butt of the holstered automatic that he had not had to touch. Then it moved to the pocket where he kept his cigarettes.

'So you didn't really need me,' he said. 'The Enriquez brothers were on the level, after their fashion. They may swindle the government and send peasants out to kill and be killed for them, but they pay their own bills. I guess there *is* honour among certain kinds of thieves.'

Doris stopped squirming and sat up with a final cathartic gasp.

'Oh, no,' she said. 'I'm glad we ran into you. Terribly glad.'

And suddenly her lips were on his mouth, hot and hungry, and her body against him and her arms winding around him, groping . . . And then just as quickly she tore herself away, back to the far side of the seat; and he looked down and saw the gleam of his own gun in her hand, pointing at him.

'You didn't have to use it,' she said, a little breathlessly. 'But I will, if you try anything. Pull over, Sherm. I've got him covered.'

6

The Saint didn't move. He gazed at her steadily, and rather sadly, while the car lost speed without any abruptness that might have spoiled her aim.

'A perfect stranger,' he said, 'a person who didn't know your sweet loyal soul, would think you were going to take a mean advantage of me – to toss me aside like an old squeezed-out toothpaste tube.'

'A perfect stranger would be right,' she said. 'It was mighty nice to have you with us while there was a real chance that the Enriquez brothers might have been planning to pull a fast one. But now we're out of that danger, you're too expensive a partner. But you can still be useful. I figure that if we leave you for them or the cops to catch, when they find out who you are they won't care so much about trying to find us.'

'That's how I thought you had it figured.'

She peered at him sharply, then gave a short grating laugh. 'You did?'

The car had stopped now, and Inkler turned around in the front seat.

'Don't let's waste any more time, Doris.'

'Hold it, Sherm. This I have got to hear!'

'You remember the lecture I promised you about your extravagant generosity, darling?' said the Saint. 'That was the tip-off. When you came and offered me a third share of a prize like this, after you'd done all the groundwork, and with you and Sherman paying all the expenses out of your end, you overplayed it to a fare-thee-well. They just don't make fairy godparents like that in the racket. If you'd offered me about twenty grand, say, just to keep my mouth shut and do this little walk-on in the last act, I might have fallen for it. But more than a hundred and sixty thousand, free and clear – that just had to be sucker bait.'

'Then why did you go for it?'

'I had to see how it would work out. And there was always an outside chance that you might just be a little crazy. But if you were a thoroughly bad girl – if you really were trying to pull something like this on the old maestro – then I'd have to teach you a lesson.'

'I'll look forward to that,' she said.

She fumbled behind her and opened the door on her side. She got out, without ever turning away from him, and held the door open, still keeping him covered. At the same time, Sherman got out his side.

'Come on outside, Saint,' she said.

'That's a fighting phrase,' Simon remarked mildly.

But he followed her out, and she made him step a little away from the car. She handled the gun like a professional, and kept a safe distance from a sudden leap.

He gave her a last chance.

'You seemed to rather like me last night, if I may be so ungentlemanly as to mention it,' he said. 'Why don't we ditch your husband instead, and start a new team?'

She shook her head.

'Not my husband,' she said. 'My brother. We only work as husband and wife because it makes a better act. I like you a lot that way, Saint, but you just aren't in the running.'

'I'm sorry,' he said.

He caught the flicker of her eyes and the almost imperceptible whisper of movement behind him at the same instant, and spun around. He saw Sherman Inkler with something like a blackjack in his right hand raised and already falling, and stepped in under it like a cat. The Saint's left came up under the man's chin with a snap like a collision of pool balls, and Sherman was probably already unconscious before the right cross that followed the uppercut slammed him against the car and dropped him at the enforced limit of his horizontal travel.

The Saint turned. And quite deliberately, Doris Inkler shot at him. He heard the click of the firing pin, but that was all.

Then he took the gun out of her hand.

'You shouldn't have done that,' he said. 'It deprives you of your last hope of sympathy. You'd have killed me if I hadn't been careful.' He was doing something to the gun and putting it back in his shoulder holster. 'You knew where I had a gun, so I knew the first thing you'd do would be to take it, so I took out the magazine while we were driving,' he explained calmly.

She spat obscenities at him, and flew at him with her fingernails, so that he had to clip her on the jaw with a loose fist, just hard enough to knock her cold for a few seconds, rather than have his last remaining pleasant memories of her ruined.

He took the aeroplane tickets, but left them some money and their tourist cards, without which they would have found it very complicated indeed to cross any Mexican border. He felt that that was pretty Saintly, considering what they would have done to him, but that would always be his weakness. Even so, their chances would be none too good.

He got into the Cadillac and drove on.

At the outskirts of Vera Cruz he stopped for long enough to peel off his moustache and rub the grey out of his hair with a handkerchief; he put the tinted glasses in his pocket. Then he drove on again, slowly, until he found himself within a couple of blocks of bright lights. He parked the car in a dark yard, took out the suitcase of loot and walked on. In a little while he found a taxi, and ordered it to drive him to the airport. He saw no need to risk going back to the Mocambo for his over-night bag: with what he carried in his hand, he could cheerfully consider everything it contained expendable. His watch told him he had just a comfortable margin of time to catch the plane.

He checked in at the ticket counter, but kept possession of the suitcase. It was a little larger than the size which passengers are normally permitted to carry with them, but the clerk was sleepy and let him get away with it. He was passed on to another official who stamped his tourist card.

Then a hand fell on his shoulder.

'You are leaving us so soon?' said Captain Carlos Xavier.

'Just for a few days,' said the Saint, with superhuman blandness. 'Some friends of mine are honeymooning in Havana, and they begged me to hop over and see them.'

Xavier nodded.

'We still have so much to talk about. Come with me.'

He took the Saint's arm and led him past the customs counter, under the eyes of the uniformed officer, through a door marked *Entrada prohibida*, and into a small shabby office. He shut the door, and pointed to the Saint's suitcase.

'You know that if you had gone on, the officer outside would have made you open that?'

'I was just figuring how much it would cost to discourage him,' said the Saint blandly, 'when you interrupted me.'

'You will let me look in it, please?'

Simon laid the case on the desk and released the locks, but did not open it. He stepped back and let Xavier raise the lid. He unbuttoned his coat, and was glad he had reloaded his gun.

Xavier stared at the money for a long time.

'I suppose this belongs to the Enriquez brothers?' he said.

'It did,' Simon replied steadily. 'But they paid it over quite voluntarily, for what they thought was a shipment of arms and ammunition for Jalisco's revolution.'

'To be supplied by the Inklers?'

It was the Saint's turn to stare.

'How did you know?'

'Why do you think I took you to Larue last night, where I knew the Enriquez brothers would be, and where I hoped the Inklers would try to contact them? If they had not done it that night, I would have taken you wherever they went the next night. Why do you think I arranged for Inkler to be delayed, until I had had time to tell you about Manuel and Pablo? Why do you think I arranged to be called away afterwards so that you would be free to observe what happened and to act as you chose? Why do you think I have never been far away from you since then, even to watching you at sea this afternoon from an aeroplane, until it got too dark? Meeting you here, of course, was easy: I knew about your reservations as soon as they were made. But you should be grateful to me, instead of wondering whether to use the gun you have under your arm.'

'Excuse me,' said the Saint, and leaned against the wall.

'I told you I was an unusual policeman,' Xavier said. 'I received word from your FBI that the Inklers were here, and what to expect from them. They have been in other Central American countries, always working on the discontented element, and usually with the story that they could influence assistance from Washington. So I knew that the Enriquez brothers would be perfect for them. I had a problem. It was my duty not to let the Inklers swindle anyone; yet I did not have much desire to protect Manuel and Pablo. That is why I was most happy that you were here. I was sure I could rely on you for a solution.'

Simon's eyes widened in a blinding smile.

'Is anything wrong with this one?'

'It is a lot of money.' Xavier pursed his lips over it judicially. 'But I have no report of any such sum being stolen. And no one has made any accusations against you. I do not see how I can prevent you leaving with it. On the other hand, I am not very well paid, and I think you owe me something.' He took out six of the neat bundles of green paper and distributed them in different pockets of his clothing. 'I should like to retire, and buy a small hotel in Fortín.'

Simon Templar drew a deep breath, and straightened up.

'One day I must visit you there,' he said.

Captain Xavier closed the suitcase, and Simon picked it up. Xavier opened another door, and the Saint found himself out on the landing field. In front of him, the first passengers were boarding the plane.

THE ROMANTIC MATRON

I

She had probably celebrated at least thirty-five birthdays, but most of them must have marked pleasant years. Now she was entering the period of life at which the sophisticated European, impervious to the adolescent fixations with which Hollywood has helped to pervert the American taste, finds a woman most attractive. She could approach it with the confidence of a figure that had ripened without ever being allowed to get out of hand, a face enhanced by the distinction of maturity, and the kind of clothes and grooming that it takes experience as well as money to acquire.

She said, in a quick breathless way: 'You're Simon Templar, aren't you? The Saint. One of the croupiers at the Tropicana told me.'

'Did he warn you not to play cards with me?' Simon asked disinterestedly.

'Silly. I'm Mrs Carrington. Beryl, to be friendly. That's all the introduction I can manage.'

'How do you do,' he said, with restrained courtesy.

She looked over her shoulder nervously, then back to him again.

'I'm not drunk,' she said. 'Please believe that. We've got to have help and I thought you might be It.'

The Saint inhaled expressionlessly through his cigarette. It was getting to be a job for an electronic computer to count the number of times he had heard some similar opening to that. And 'help' usually meant something basically unlawful, with a good chance of getting shot, or clapped in jail, or both, as the most obvious reward.

Which was perhaps why he had had to learn to draw a mask over the glints of purely juvenile devilment that always tended to creep into his eyes at such inspiriting prospects.

'What's the matter?' he inquired patiently. 'Did you lose your husband, or are you trying to?'

'Please be serious. I've only got a moment.'

He had all the time in the world, but he had been toying with the preposterous whimsy that he might be able to spend some of it in Havana without any of the things happening to him that seemed to happen everywhere else.

He flicked over in his mind the other times he had seen her. Because of course he had noticed her, as she had noticed him.

The first time, two days ago, in the Capitolio Nacional.

Simon Templar would not ordinarily have been a customer for a piece of conducted sightseeing, especially of a government building, and least of all one which from the outside promised to be just another version of the central-domed design which has become the architectural cliché of the Capitols of the New World. But a taxi driver had mentioned that set in the floor under the dome there was a diamond worth fifty thousand dollars, and this he was curious to see. After all, although the days were somewhat precariously past when he would have been thinking seriously of stealing it, he did not have to forgo the intellectual exercise of casing the job and figuring out how it might be done.

That was the only reason why he happened to be one of a small group of tourists shuffling through the Salon de los Pasos Perdidos, listening with half an ear to the recitation of the guide ('*The Hall of Lost Footsteps ... largest in the world ... four hundred feet ... Florentine Renaissance style. Please notice how the pattern of the ceiling is exactly reproduced in the tile on the floor . . .'*) and then gawking up at the immense symbolic gilt figure of The Republic (*'The biggest indoor statue in the world . . . the spear alone weighs a ton . . .'*) and finally clustered with them around the small roped-off square in the centre of which was the diamond (*'Bought with the contributions of everyone who worked on this building . . . It marks the exact spot from which all distances in Cuba are measured. When they say it is a hundred miles to Havana, and you wonder what part of Havana they mean, this is the place . . . it has thirty-two facets, the same as the number of points of the compass . . .'*). But you had to take the guide's word for it, for all you could see was a small circular brass grating set in the floor with a pane of glass under it, through which you could only imagine that you saw a diamond.

So the Saint let his gaze shift idly over the faces of his fellow tourists, and the one that arrested it was Mrs Carrington's. Hers first because it was notably easy to look at on its own merits; and then in conjunction with and emphasized by the face of the man with her, who kept a possessive hand under her arm. For just as she was unmistakably a visitor, with her Nordic features and colouring, the man with his well-oiled black hair and olive skin and rather long-nosed good looks was no less obviously a Cuban. The oddity, of course, being that you would never normally expect to find a native of Havana among such a typical clutch of rubber-necks. He didn't look a day older than the woman, which left just enough room for cynical speculation to impress them both on the Saint's memory. Simon found himself dawdling towards the rear of the sightseeing party as it was ushered out of the building, being vaguely inquisitive about what the couple might reveal in the manner of their departure, and saw them get into a new Mercury that was parked outside. It had Indiana licence plates, but the man drove it.

And shortly after that Simon would probably have let

them disappear into the limbo of all fruitless surmises. But before he could forget them, he saw them again.

The second time, the night before, at the Tropicana.

The Tropicana claims to be the biggest and the most beautiful night club in the world. It is indeed enormously big; and its fine-weather auditorium, roofed only by the sky and colonnaded with glamorously lighted palm trees, is certainly quite a sight. But in spite of the spectacular advantage of a backdrop of living trees interlaced with spidery stairways and catwalks over which the chorus was able to make endless dramatic entrances, countermarches, and exits, the floor show was tremendous without much leavening of inspiration, and Simon was finally glad to vacate his seat at the bar and edge his way laboriously through the crowd to the Casino. And there she sat at the roulette table, with the same man standing behind her chair.

The Saint's analytical eyes observed that she played without strain, moderately disappointed when she lost, reasonably elated when she won, but always relaxed enough to exchange a smiling word now and then with her companion. Therefore her luck was not financially important to her. But he also noted that her stakes were quite modest; and that, combined with the knowledge he already had that her car was not the most expensive make on the market, suggested that she was no more than comfortably well off, without the astronomical kind of bank balance that one automatically associates with such extravagances as gigolos. Could it then be a more genuine romance? There were well-heeled men in Cuba, too, and she was undeniably an attractive woman. But he saw her pick up a small stack of chips and offer them to the man, clearly urging him to play with them; the man shook his head in firm but amiable refusal. Then they both seemed to feel the Saint watching them, and looked at him, and he moved away. It could never be any great concern of his, anyhow – he thought.

Until now.

The croupier had nodded to him as he passed, he remembered, saying helpfully, 'Not going to Puerto Rico this winter, sir?' – and the Saint had shrugged with affable vagueness and moved on before he placed the man, but realized that they must have seen each other across a table somewhere in San Juan. So it was probably true that that was how Beryl Carrington had learned his name.

But now she introduced herself as Mrs Carrington; and it was at least certain, for the record, that a man with the looks of her steady companion could not possibly be Mr Carrington.

It could well have seemed like a stretch of coincidence when the Saint strolled in to the Bambú that night and found himself seated two tables away from them. Yet the Bambú, billed as a typically Cuban night spot, was just as ineluctably as the Tropicana on the itinerary of any tourist who was stubbornly determined (as the Saint had been) to find out, regardless of the trauma to his pocketbook and eardrums, exactly what was the legendary fascination of Havana. But this time they had seen him at once, and turned to each other as unanimously as if their heads had been geared together, very evidently to talk about it.

Simon had tried his best this time to suggest innocence of any intention. Perhaps almost too studiously, he had kept his gaze from returning even approximately in their direction. And so now she was sitting beside him, asking for some nebulous kind of help.

It could do no more damage to look towards her table now, so he did, and saw that her boy friend was no longer sitting there.

'He went to the men's room,' she said. 'I can't say much now, because I don't want him to catch me. I'm not sure he'd like it.'

'Shouldn't you have found that out before you risked getting a knife stuck in me?' Simon murmured.

'I'm staying at the Comodoro. Mrs Carrington. Will you call me tomorrow? Any time. Please.' Again her eyes took a furtive glance around, and then they came back to him with an entreaty as urgent as the breathlessness of her voice. 'Please, please do. I must go now.'

And before he could make any answer she was back at her own table, completely absorbed in the manipulation of mirror and lipstick. Her entire absence had been so brief that anyone who had not been watching her like a hawk might never have noticed that she had moved at all.

Simon Templar managed to look equally nonchalant as he took a long pull at his drink.

The orchestra, which had been mercifully silent during the bare minute that Beryl Carrington's visit had taken, splintered the ephemeral lull with a blast of saxophones hurled full blast at the microphones which Cuban musical taste requires to be placed only inches away from the loudest sections of any orchestra; and in another instant a typically tuneless bedlam of brass was in full frenzied swing, amplified to bone-bruising intensity through the battery of souped-up loud speakers which Cuban custom demands for disseminating music through even the smallest room, and pounded remorselessly home with an assortment of drums, cymbals, rattles, gourds full of dried seeds, and just plain pieces of wood beaten together. Under the impact of that jungle cacophony magnified to the maximum intensity attainable through the abuse of modern electronics, the Saint found it relatively easy to keep his face a blank. In fact, about all he had to do was to let it mirror the numbness which the blare and concussion was threatening to induce in his brain. But out of the corner of his eye he saw Mrs Carrington's playmate return to their table, and speak to her without sitting down; and she stood up, and they moved on to the dance floor and wedged themselves in among the dedicated crowd who were wriggling and jostling through the motions of a rumba or samba or mambo or whatever the current terpsichorean aphrodisiac was being called that season with every appearance of enjoyment.

About that time Simon Templar decided that he never was likely to experience for himself the mystic rapture which is evoked in some persons by Afro-Hispanic minstrelsy. Something in his cosmogony had undoubtedly been lacking from birth, and he decided to get out while he still had a few other faculties left, before the stupefying din left permanent scar tissue among his brain cells. He had to escape from that paralysing pandemonium to be able to make up his mind about Mrs Carrington's peculiar invitation anyhow, and there could be no more inconspicuous time to do it than while she and her dancing partner were submerged in the gyrating mob in front of the bandstand. He succeeded in catching a waiter's eye, and made the pantomime of scribbling on the palm of one raised flat hand which is understood to request a bill anywhere in the world.

As he emerged into the relative quiet outside, the doorman and three loitering drivers vocally offered taxi service, but they were physically cut out by a broad butterball of a man who half encircled the Saint's back with a brotherly arm and grinned: 'I got the best car for you, sir, and the best price.'

For just long enough to let himself be steered diagonally across the driveway into the parking lot, Simon submitted tolerantly to what seemed to be merely the effective technique of the most determined salesman on the beat. Then as he realized that they had gone just a little too far from the entrance, and a corner had shut them off from the sight of anyone there, the man stopped and turned him quite violently, and Simon looked down at the gleam of a knife-blade in the gloom.

'How long do you stay in Cuba, *señor*?' asked the man.

'Only as long as I can stand the noise,' snapped the Saint.

The fat man's teeth flashed in the same dim light that glinted on the steel in his hand. Even at that distance the music was so loud that it must certainly prevent anyone around the entrance of the club from hearing almost anything that might happen in the parking lot, short of an atomic explosion.

'I think you will go home tomorrow,' the man said, 'if you don't want to get hurt. People don't like you to spy on them. You are just a nuisance.'

'Well, Pancho,' said the Saint judicially, 'speaking purely on the spur of the moment, I should say you were just a horse's ass.'

And then, as the fat man's patronizing grin vanished, he moved with a speed that the other, for all his apparent professionalism, could never have allowed for. That fat man himself could never reconstruct exactly what happened; he only knew that a blow out of nowhere sapped all the strength from his fingers, and that the knife he dropped was caught in mid-air almost as he released it and presented point first at the tip of his own nose.

'Go back to the goat who sent you,' said the Saint, in fluent Spanish, 'and tell him that it annoys me to be rushed. And when I am annoyed, I do things like this.'

The stout man flinched from the flash of metal across his eyes as the knife spun away into the night. And then a fist that felt no less metallic, although blunter, impinged crisply on his nose and sat him down suddenly in his tracks with a new constellation of lights zipping across his vision. Before he could clear his involuntarily streaming eyes, the Saint was no longer in sight.

In a taxi heading back towards town along the Rancho Boyeros highway, the driver said helpfully: 'You no have a girl tonight, sir?'

'Not tonight,' said the Saint.

'You are smart guy, I think. Some women you find make much trouble . . . But if you like, if you are lonely, I have young cousin, very honest and beautiful girl—'

'Thank you,' Simon said. 'But I think someone just got an option on me.'

2

'You see,' Beryl Carrington told him, 'Ramón is one of the top men in the Underground.'

'Oh,' said the Saint; and now for the first time he did begin to see a little.

She jumped up restlessly, with a swirl of the clinging négligé that she had put on when he knocked.

'It's exciting, and rather frightening – isn't it? – to think that things like that still have to go on, and so close to the United States.'

'Sure,' he said. 'But how does it happen to concern you?'

She stared at him, puzzled and almost hurt.

'If I hadn't heard it, I wouldn't have believed that the Saint asked that question. Isn't the fight for freedom, anywhere, something that concerns all of us these days?'

'I know the oratory,' Simon said mildly. 'I meant – why you, personally?'

'I got into it when I met Ramón.'

'Where did you meet him? Here?'

'Yes.'

'What part of Indiana are you from?'

'Why, is the accent so obvious?'

'No, but your car plates are. Excuse me if I sound like a district attorney, but I like to know just a few things about the people I'm supposed to help.'

'I understand.' She sat down, facing him. 'Prewisburg, Indiana, is the place. Probably you've never heard of it, it's a very small town. I was born and raised there, and I lived there all my life. This is the farthest away I've ever been. I married my high-school sweetheart, who was also the heir to the biggest industry in town – an umbrella factory. You don't look like a man who ever owned an umbrella, but if you had one it could easily be a Carrington. They're very good umbrellas. My husband was a very good guy and a good husband – and just as dull as an umbrella. We had a good, comfortable, normal, and very dull life. Until he died of a good dull case of lobar pneumonia a couple of years ago. It wasn't until I got over that that I realized how very ordinary and how very dull my entire life had been. I wasn't left filthy rich – that wouldn't have been ordinary, would it? – but I could afford to go anywhere within reason. So I decided to see a few places while I was still young enough to have fun. Does that tell you enough?'

Simon nodded, and poured himself another cup of coffee – she had been having breakfast in her room when he arrived, and had ordered a fresh pot of coffee for him.

'And here you just happened to meet Ramón.'

'It wasn't exactly that kind of pick-up,' she said.

Beryl Carrington had been told by a travel agent that if she wanted to see more of Cuba than the city of Havana where all the tourists go, it would be cheaper to have her own car ferried over from Key West. She had faced the prospect of trying to find her way around in a foreign country with some trepidation, but had finally decided to let it be an adventure. By the time she reached her hotel after getting lost five times on her way from the dock she was wondering whether that kind of adventure could possibly be worth any economy it effected; and a call on the house phone that came to her room while she was still unpacking convinced her that she could only have fallen for the idea during a spell of mental incompetence.

'I am very sorry,' the caller said, 'but I have had a little accident to your car.'

Ramón Venino, as he introduced himself with a card in the lobby, was very apologetic and very embarrassed. She was too upset at first to notice how very personable he also was.

'My hand slipped on the wheel – but that is no excuse. I was careless. I wish to take all responsibility.'

They went out together to the parking area to inspect the damage, which consisted of one moderately crumpled fender.

'It is only a little less bad because it is easy to fix,' Venino said. 'Give me the key, and I will take it to a garage, and tonight I will bring it back like new.'

Very quickly and sharply she visualized herself waiting from then until Domesday to see either him or her car again. She was distinctly pleased with her own poise and perspicacity.

'Thanks,' she said. 'I'd rather take it to a garage myself.'

He inclined his head.

'As you wish. The hotel manager will recommend a place. I only insist that I pay the bill.'

After she had been directed to a garage, and was faced only with the navigational problem of actually finding it, she found Venino waiting beside her car with a taxi.

'Tell the driver where you are going,' he said, 'and he will lead the way. He speaks good English, and he will help you at the garage. Then he will drive you where you want to go for the rest of the day. Don't pay him anything – it is all taken care of.'

He bowed, and left her before she could think of anything to say.

The next morning, however, she recognized his voice when it spoke on the house telephone again.

'Please don't be annoyed that I have brought your car back myself,' he said. 'I only wish to be sure that you are completely satisfied with the repair before I pay the garage.'

The fender had been so well smoothed out and repainted that it would have taken a magnifying glass to find fault with it. And the fact remained that Venino had apparently had little difficulty in persuading the garage to turn the car over to him. If he had been a car thief with a new angle, as her hypertrophied caution had at first suspected him, he could already have got away with his objective.

'It looks fine,' she said.

'I can only apologize again for the inconvenience,' he said. 'I am sorry we could not have met in any other way, so that I could have hoped to see you again without you thinking bad things of me.'

It was her turn to feel awkward and embarrassed.

'I think you've been very charming,' she said. 'If everyone who had an accident was like you, the insurance companies would be out of business.'

'You are very kind. But still I have made it impossible for me ever to ask you to dinner.'

His manner was studiously correct but disarmingly wistful, and his good looks were finally able to make their impression on her.

'Don't be silly,' she said. 'Why not ask me, and let me decide how I feel?'

He had given her the most enjoyable evening she had yet spent in Havana, and had distinguished himself further by not making a single premature pass. Therefore she had no excuse for refusing to let him drive her around sightseeing in her own car the next day – which prolonged itself painlessly into another dinner together, and thus into another project for the following morning. And so on.

Almost from the first evening she began to notice odd things about him – the way he would stop and look carefully up and down the street every time they came out of a building, a trick of glancing back over his shoulder at unexpected moments, his phobia about taking any table in a restaurant where he could not sit facing the entrance and with his back to a wall, the continual restless wandering of his eyes. By the third day she had no hesitation about asking him why.

'And so he told you,' said the Saint.

'I suppose it was easier for him, since I was a foreigner, so at least he could be pretty sure I wasn't already on the other side. And we'd become very good friends very quickly. You know, that can happen.'

Simon nodded.

'What is he afraid of?'

'You forget, it's really a dictatorship here. And Ramón is one of the people who are trying to get rid of the Strong Man and bring democracy back. You know what would happen to him if the Secret Police caught him.'

'I'm afraid I haven't been following Cuban politics too closely,' Simon confessed. 'However, what's the programme for getting rid of the Strong Man? A fine rowdy revolution, or a nice neat assassination?'

'Neither,' she said with some spirit. 'Ramón and his friends aren't gangsters. You can't build a lasting good government on any kind of violence. And it isn't necessary, either. The majority *wants* freedom, as they do in any dictatorship. They're just held down by one small group that's well organized and has all the key positions. So the Underground is organizing too, and they'll just arrest that group all at once, the same as a surgeon would remove a growth, without chopping the patient up with an axe.'

'It sounds frightfully humane and tidy,' Simon remarked. 'South American revolutions were a lot more fun when I was a boy. So time marches on . . . Well, when is this change-over set for?'

'Very soon now. It might be almost any day.'

'If it's all so efficiently organized and ready to roll so soon, I'm still wondering why you so desperately need me.'

She stood up again, as if the springs of repressed excitement would not let her relax.

'They're afraid that there may be a traitor in the Underground.'

'Aha.'

'And if there is, he might know that Ramón is the only man who has a complete list of all the members. You see what that means? If Ramón was arrested by the Secret Police, everything would be lost. He's sure that they'd never get a single name out of him under any torture' – she shuddered – 'but if they got the list, all his courage wouldn't make any difference.'

'I'm beginning to appreciate this lad Ramón,' said the Saint. 'The list, I gather, isn't in his head.'

'Of course not. It couldn't possibly be. There are thousands of names and addresses on it. Naturally there *has* to be one key list like that; but can you imagine the responsibility of trying to keep it safe?'

Simon regarded her steadily.

'Looking at you,' he observed thoughtfully, 'I gather that it makes you pretty jittery.'

She stared at him, her eyes widening and her mouth falling open.

'I didn't say—'

'No, you didn't say it, darling. But my brain is beginning to work. Obviously, Ramón has asked you to take care of this list.'

She brought her lips together again with a shrug of resolution.

'All right, that's it. I'm leaving tonight, and I'm to take it back to the States with me. I can put it in a safe deposit box in Miami until Ramón needs it, and the Secret Police can't do anything about that.'

'But you're scared about getting it there – is that it? You've been seen around with Ramón too much. If he's already being watched – which you don't know – then you may be suspected yourself.'

'Ramón thinks the odds are on my side. As an American who's never been here before, they ought to believe I'm . . . well, just a passing romance. But I can't help thinking and thinking about the other possibility. Suppose they *don't*?'

'You've got something to worry about.'

'So that's why – when I saw you for the third time running last night – and by that time I knew who you were – it seemed like an omen. I had to ask you for help.' In her intensity she was completely sexless, either because she scorned such wiles or because nothing in her background was consonant with the use of them; yet for that very reason her appeal was stronger than any siren could have achieved. 'Please, will you?'

'Yes,' said the Saint calmly.

She slumped against the wall, twisting her hands together.

'I feel so stupid and small,' she said. 'And I was so excited at first. Coming here, and meeting a man who turned out to be a real hero like Ramón and winning his confidence. And then having the chance to do something really important for the first time in my life – something truly dangerous and romantic, like most people only read about. But when it came right to the point, I found I didn't have what it takes. It wasn't only being scared of how I'd react to being arrested, or – or the things they might do to me. It was thinking of the thousands of other people whose lives I'd be responsible for. And I found out I was in a blue frozen funk, all through my insides . . . You must despise me.'

'Anything but. I'm glad you had the sense to know when you were out of your depth, and the guts to admit it.' The Saint's brows lowered over a passing thought. 'Ramón spotted me last night, too – I saw you speak to each other about it. What did he say?'

'He didn't like it. I told him it must be a coincidence, and you couldn't possibly be against him, but he was worried. I tried to tell him what everyone knows about you, but I don't know how much I convinced him. That's why I still haven't told him I spoke to you.'

Simon lighted a cigarette.

'All right. Where is this list now?'

'It's in one of my suitcases. He left it with me last night.'

She hesitated a moment, and then went and opened a suitcase which stood on a trestle in a corner. She turned over a few folded pieces of clothing and brought out an alligator briefcase.

She came over to the Saint with it, and he took it.

'What's the opposite of a nightmare?' she said. 'It's the word I need for the way it feels to know I don't have to think twice about trusting you.'

'The words you're thinking of may be "pipe-dream",' he said sardonically.

The briefcase was brand new, so that the leather bulged stiffly over the bulk that it contained. It was equipped with a lock which Simon recognized as being much more resistant to amateur picking than the average run of such hardware, although of course it had no defence against a sharp knife in the hands of anyone who was not bothered about preserving its virginal appearance.

'I'd suggest you go on packing, and let Ramón think this is still in the bottom of that suitcase – then there won't be any argument,' said the Saint, and got to his feet. 'By the way, when are you seeing him again?'

'He's coming here at one o'clock, for a farewell lunch – or I suppose you'd say, an *hasta la vista*. He has to bring my car back, anyhow – I let him take it home last night after he brought me back, because his own car is in the shop having an overhaul.'

The Saint's very clear blue eyes searched her face with disconcerting penetration.

'You think a lot of this guy, don't you?'

'Only because of what he's doing, and what he stands for,' she insisted. 'I'm not a middle-aged sugar-mammy who came here to look for a Latin thrill. You mustn't believe that.'

'I don't,' he said soberly. 'And most especially the "middle-aged" part.'

He stubbed out his cigarette and turned towards the door.

'Thanks to the discretion ingrained in me by a misspent youth,' he said, 'I got out of my taxi two blocks away, walked over to the beach, wandered into the back of this *posada* by way of the swimming pool, and ambled up a service stair-way. If any Gestapo gunsels do happen to be watching you, I don't think they saw me coming and I don't think they'll see me leave.'

'But where'll I see you again?' she gasped, in a sudden panic.

'If you don't know, nobody can make you tell. But I'll find you. Don't worry.' He grinned, and tapped the briefcase under his arm. 'Whatever happens, I shall be holding the bag.'

He had already started down the service stairs when he heard other footsteps coming up. It was too late to turn back, for whoever was coming up would have turned the corner of the half-landing and seen him before he could have retreated out of sight, and his abrupt reversal of direction would have looked guilty even to someone who was quite unsuspicious. And there was no reason why the feet could not belong to innocent guests of the hotel or its equally inoffensive employees. Simon kept on going, with his reflexes triggered on invisible needle points.

They were two men in dark suits, with a certain air about

them which to the Saint was as informative as a label. They looked at him with mechanical curiosity, but he held his course without faltering, and they fell into single file to let him go by. He passed them with the smile and carefree nod of a tourist who had never consciously noticed a policeman in plain clothes in his life.

As he reached the foot of the stairs, the voice of one of them came down to him from the floor above, speaking low and tersely in Spanish.

'Hide yourself here, and take note of anyone who comes to visit her.'

3

Out there in the Miramar district where the Comodoro Hotel is located, Havana's Fifth Avenue (which, like Manhattan's Sixth, has been officially re-christened 'Avenue of the Americas,' and is just as stubbornly known only by its old name to every native) is far from being the city's busiest thoroughfare, and as he reached it Simon was wondering if he would have trouble finding a taxi. He did not want to be wandering around the streets of that neighbourhood for long, where not only might the plain-clothes men he had already encountered decide belatedly to investigate him, but Ramón Venino might come driving by from any direction en route to his rendezvous with Beryl Carrington.

He need have had no anxiety. He had barely taken one glance up and down the street when a taxi, drawn by the uncanny instinct for prey that achieves its supreme development in the vulture and the Havana taxi driver, made a screaming U turn and swooped in to the curb beside him.

'Where to?' asked the driver cheerily, starting off without waiting to find out. 'Are you hoping to meet a girl, or is your wife here with you? I have a young sister, a lovely girl, but very naughty, who is crazy for Americanos.'

'I have a weak heart,' said the Saint, 'and the doctor has ordered me to leave naughty girls alone.'

'Some sightseeing then? I can take you to the Botanical Gardens, then to the Cathedral—'

Simon frowned at the briefcase on the seat beside him.

Wherever he went, its pristine newness would be conspicuous; and to walk into his hotel with it in full view, where either policemen or friends of the man he had called Pancho might be watching for him, would be too naïve to even consider.

'How about one of the rum distilleries?' he suggested.

'Yes, sir. I will take you to Trocadero.'

Presently they drew up beside a large low building, at an entrance with sliding doors designed for trucks to drive through. The driver waved aside the Saint's proffered payment.

'I will be here when you come out.'

Simon stepped into the odorous interior, and was adopted at once by the nearest of a number of men who stood waiting by the entrance.

'Good morning, sir. This is where we make that famous Cuban rum. Step this way, please.' They entered one corner of a vast barn-like factory. 'The sugar cane is pulped in that machine there, and then the juice is fermented in those tanks over there. Then it passes through those stills which you see there, and the rum goes into those barrels to be aged. Now this way, please.' They passed through another door into a large room conveniently at hand, where there were several tables already well populated by other visitors concluding their research into the manufacture of rum. 'Here we invite you to sample our products. Sit down and be comfortable – there is no hurry.'

Each table was provided with stools on three sides and a long row of bottles on the fourth. Simon's guide went behind the bottles and at once became a bartender rapidly pouring samples into an inexhaustible supply of glasses, as other guides all over the room were already doing for their personal protégés.

'This is our light rum, this is our dark rum, this is our very best rum. Don't be bashful, it's all on the house. These are our liqueurs – apricot brandy, blackberry brandy, crème de cacao. Have whatever you want, there is no limit. And you should try our special exotic drinks – banana cordial, pineapple cordial, mango cordial. You are allowed to take back five bottles with you free of duty. Would you like some of our Tropical Punch, or some Elixir, or a frozen Daiquiri?'

'I'll take five bottles of plain drinking rum,' said the Saint, sipping very judiciously. 'But I want 'em in one of those fancy baskets that you give away.'

'Of course.' The man whipped out a pad and wrote the order. 'I'll get them for you right away. Help yourself to anything you want while you're waiting.'

Simon moistened his tongue experimentally, out of academic interest, with some of the more unfamiliar flavours; but he was in no mood, as most of the students of distillation around him seemed to be, to take memorable advantage of the phenomenon of unlimited free drinks. He was not even interested in the rum he was buying, except as much of it as would be suitable ballast for the container it would come in.

The guide-salesman returned promptly, bearing a sturdy straw bag of the kind in which every island in the Caribbean makes a trade-mark of packaging the homing tourist's duty-free quota of the local brew. Simon paid him, picked up the bag along with the briefcase which he had brought in with him, and went out to look for his driver, who had expected to rack up a nice hunk of waiting time and was disappointed to see him so soon.

'Take me to the Sevilla-Baltimore,' said the Saint.

He quietly removed the paper-wrapped bottles from the straw bag, and put the new alligator briefcase in.

'Do you drink rum, *amigo*?' Simon inquired.

'Sometimes,' said the driver indifferently.

Simon handed a bottle over the back of the front seat.

'Put this away for when you feel thirsty,' he said.

'Thank you, *señor*,' said the driver, much more brightly. 'Did you enjoy the distillery?'

'It was most educational,' said the Saint. He passed over another bottle. 'Take this one home to your sister, the lovely and naughty one, with my compliments and regrets.'

'I thank you for her,' said the driver earnestly. 'She would certainly be crazy for an Americano like you. It is a great pity your heart is not just a little stronger. She can be most gentle, too.'

'It would be a privilege to die in her arms,' Simon said gravely, 'but it might be embarrassing for you both.'

The three remaining bottles, replaced alongside and over-lapping the briefcase, adequately concealed it and left the straw bag bulging just about the same as before.

'I will wait for you,' said the driver, as Simon got out in front of the hotel.

'Not this time,' Simon told him firmly. 'I may not go out again today at all.'

He let the distillery basket be snatched by a determined bellhop, and followed it up the steps to the lobby after paying off the cab.

'What room, sir?'

'Can you keep it down here for me till I check out?' Simon asked, and added for the conclusive benefit of anyone who might be listening: 'I don't want to start drinking it up before I get home.'

The bellhop took the bag to the little store room behind the bell captain's desk, and gave him the stub of a tag. Simon gave him a quarter in exchange and strolled casually away towards the elevators; but as he reached the elevator alcove he swung briskly to his left around a group of visiting fire-men and turned off again down the little-used passage to the side entrance on the Prado. But it was not too little used for there to be a taxi waiting outside, and Simon was in it before the driver had time to deliver more than the first four words of his sales talk.

'The Toledo,' Simon said.

'If you want a real good restaurant,' said the driver, 'let me take you to—'

'I have to meet someone at the Toledo – and,' Simon continued rapidly, to forestall any further suggestions, 'she happens to be a young and beautiful girl.'

This was the purest fiction; but he had nevertheless picked the Toledo for a reason. He had eaten well enough there once before, and knew it to be a small quiet place that made relatively little effort to invite the tourist trade. He thought that he might have done a fair job of throwing any possible followers off his scent for a while, and he did not want to show himself in any of the places where the blood-hounds would most naturally go sniffing first if they were trying to get back on his trail. At least he would like a chance to enjoy his lunch, and a breathing spell in which to sit still and think.

He ordered a dish of Moro crab, that big-clawed delicacy who manages somehow to be just a little more succulent down there than his brother the stone crab of the Florida keys, and a paella Valenciana, and said, 'One other thing – do you think you can find a newspaper lying around anywhere?'

'I will see,' said the waiter.

Simon lighted a cigarette and sipped a glass of manzanilla, and began to take a few things apart in his mind.

Just as positively as the two men he had seen at the Comodoro were of the police, the man he had called Pancho was not. Simon had yet to meet any kind of police, even Secret Police, who threatened people with knives. And if the short man had had any kind of authority, the Saint would never have got away with punching him in the nose. Simon had made no effort to disappear that night, and it wouldn't have taken a determined search very long to locate him among Havana's relatively few hotels.

But by the same token it wouldn't have taken Pancho's mob much longer to do the same thing, if they had any sort of organization.

Simon had assumed that Pancho was under orders of Venino. Had Mrs Carrington's argument, then, finally convinced Venino that the Saint meant no danger to him, and had Venino called Pancho off?

That was what Venino might well be hoping that the Saint would believe. But the Saint didn't believe it for one moment. To believe it, he would have had to accept two or three much greater improbabilities that he simply could not buy.

There had to be some other explanation that would tie everything together; and whatever it was, it could only be as illegitimate as a cardinal's daughter.

The waiter brought the Moro crab claws, and with them a slightly rumpled copy of *Informacion*.

'*Lo siento*, it is all we have. But if you like I can send out for a Miami paper.'

'No, this is what I wanted.' Simon looked at him with a lift of the eyebrows that was as expressive as it was calculated. 'But do you mean to say that you can get Miami papers here?'

The waiter's surprise was manifestly unfeigned.

'Yes, why not?'

'Even if they say rude things about the President?'

The waiter shrugged.

'What President is not criticized somewhere, *señor*?'

'Do you ever criticize him?' Simon asked.

'I do not argue about politics,' said the other cheerfully. 'It is like religion. It is easy to offend someone and very hard to convert anyone.'

'But you aren't afraid that if you said what you thought you might land in the *juzgado*.'

The waiter looked honestly puzzled.

'What would the President care what a poor waiter said?'

'Then you aren't looking forward to a revolution,' Simon said.

The waiter laughed.

'I hope not. Revolutions are bad for business.'

The Saint let him go to attend to another table, and proceeded to read the newspaper with unusual assiduousness while he ate.

For once he was uninterested in any international events, but he read every line that had any reference to local affairs. And although he did not skip any political items, he was most hopeful of finding the missing link that he needed under much more sensational headlines. A major jewel robbery would have suited him very well – or, as a supreme refinement of plot construction, it would have been almost deliriously intoxicating to read that some ingenious sportsman had actually contrived to steal from the Capitol the diamond across which he had first set eyes on Beryl Carrington and Ramón Venino. But nothing as poetic as that rewarded him – in fact, the only important larceny he found mentioned was an armoured carload of bullion which seemed to have recently vanished somehow between the Banco Insular and the Treasury, which the police were still looking for. And even if some Underground of self-convinced patriots had pulled that caper, it certainly was not hidden in an alligator briefcase.

Suddenly the Saint realized that it no longer made sense to be so coy about that briefcase.

He watched the waiter place beside his coffee cup the complimentary glass of coffee liqueur topped with cream which is the custom of the country, and said, 'You have converted me, *amigo*. I have decided against the revolution. My bill, please.'

'*Si, señor.*'

Fifteen minutes later he was at the Prado entrance of the Sevilla-Biltmore again, this time on his way in. He turned immediately towards the elevators, and caught one that was just about to start up. Out of an ingrained habit of preparedness he had his key in his pocket and had not needed to go to the desk for it, and there was nobody lurking around his landing that he could see as he let himself into his room. He went straight to the telephone and called the bell captain.

'Have the goodness to send up the bag of rum which I left down there,' he said, and gave the number of his claim check.

He hung up, and as he did so he heard the sound behind him, though it was no more than the faintest scuff of fabric or the catch of an over-restrained breath. But it made the difference that he was turning as the blanket fell over his head, and the man who threw it did not clamp him quite solidly in the bear-hug that was meant to pinion it over his arms. Another pair of arms clutched him around the knees in the next instant, and he was lifted off his feet and being carried swiftly across the room; he could feel the direction and an involuntary chill went through him, but he went on squirming and lifting his elbows outwards and freed his arms enough to drive one fist after another into something that sobbed and yielded. The grip around his shoulders weakened, and he brought his knees up towards his chest and kicked out again savagely and felt his heels crunch satisfyingly against flesh and bone, and then he was free and falling only a little way to the floor.

The blanket fell off him as he thrashed up, and he saw that he was right beside the open window and in another moment no doubt would have been falling out of it. A queasy horror in his stomach transformed him into a bolt of berserk lightning that completed the annulment of the two men who would have done it to him before they could comprehend the catastrophic extent of their failure. The big man who had thrown the blanket, who was still bent double over what the Saint's punches had done to his mid-section, took a kick in the face that dropped him in an inert heap; and Pancho the fat boy, who was holding his ribs with one hand and bringing out his switch-knife with the other, only felt the first of the two teak-like fists that bounced his head off the wall until his folding knees took it down below easy reach . . .

Simon Templar stood breathing slowly and deeply, and gradually became aware of a prosaic but persistent knocking on the door.

He walked over to it, past the open closet where he realized Pancho and his taller pal must have been waiting for him, and flung the door open. A bellboy with the rum basket in one hand stared at him and then beyond him with bulging eyes.

Simon took the bag from him before he dropped it, and acknowledged the two facsimiles of corpses on the floor with a deprecatory gesture.

'They attacked me and tried to rob me,' he said casually. 'Send for a policeman to take them away, *por favor.*'

The lad turned and scooted away like a startled rabbit.

Simon sat on the bed and picked up the telephone again. While he waited for the operator to answer, he extracted the briefcase from under the bottles in the bag.

'The Hotel Comodoro,' he requested.

Reaching out a long leg, he raked Pancho's knife across the floor towards him, and picked it up. He held the telephone between his ear and his hunched shoulder while he turned the briefcase over and inserted the point of the knife delicately into a seam.

'Mrs Carrington, please,' he said to the Comodoro operator.

It was like a cue for background music when she answered almost at once.

'Beryl,' he said, 'this is Simon Templar. Just answer yes or no. Is Ramón with you?'

'Yes,' she said. 'I just finished packing.'

'Pretend I'm your travel agency checking with you. Does he still think you've got the briefcase?'

'Yes. I'll be driving straight to New York, and then probably going to Europe.'

Simon gazed down at what the briefcase had spilled into his lap through the seam he had slit open. It was nothing but an old Havana telephone directory.

'Don't move from there, and keep Ramón with you,' he said. 'Tell him I have to verify your engine number before I can get you a boarding pass for the ferry. Don't try to argue. The click you will hear will be me taking off.'

He put the phone down in its bracket and was on his way.

4

He went down a back stairway which he had taken note of the very first time he left his room – it was another habit he would probably never lose, that in any new surroundings he automatically and unconsciously observed the alternative and less obvious exits. The police would inevitably ride up in an elevator; and even though he might never have a better chance to play the outraged innocent victim, he would inevitably pay for it with an involvement in red tape that might keep him tied up for hours, and he figured that that could wait. The police would catch up with him soon enough now.

Pancho and his big brother had caught up with him, after all. In a hotel with the Grand Central atmosphere of the Sevilla-Biltmore, no one would have noticed them going up to the Saint's floor; the old-fashioned lock on his door would not have delayed them for more than ten seconds; and, but for their grievous miscalculation of his superlatively vigilant senses and tigerish fighting power, no one would have noticed them leaving after the Saint had become a splash on the pavement seventy feet down from his window.

So for a little while he could give a shocking surprise to anyone who was relying on the efficiency of Pancho and Pal.

He slipped through the service crypts of the hotel without encountering anybody but one belatedly perplexed *camarero*, and with no trouble found a door that let him out into an alley lined with garbage cans, and thus in a few more steps he was on a side street looking for a taxi, and as usual there was a taxi waiting for him.

In her room, Mrs Carrington put down the phone and said: 'That was the travel agency. They have to send someone over to verify the engine number of my car so I can get a pass to go on the ferry.'

'Is that all?' Venino said. 'You looked so troubled, I thought it was something serious.'

'It's just a nuisance.'

'It will be all right.' He frowned. 'But it seems so foolish. They could check your engine number at the dock.'

She shrugged.

'Anyway, the agency's taking care of it. But when your people take over, you should make them fire all the bureaucrats who invent stupid regulations. Just think, you could go down to history as the man who created the first government in the world to abolish red tape.'

'What I am doing is nothing to joke about.'

He spoke so roughly that it was like being physically pushed aside.

'I'm sorry.'

'Forgive me,' he said quickly. 'I am on edge. I am more afraid all the time that something is going wrong. Those men . . .'

When Ramón Venino had arrived and called up from the lobby to announce himself, and she had left her room to go down and meet him, she had quite accidentally looked directly at a face that was looking directly towards her through the two-inch opening of a door at the end of the corridor. It was more discomfiting because the man did not move or look away before she did, apparently believing himself invisible, and she could feel his eyes on her back all the way to the elevator.

Then, when they went to the bar for a cocktail, there was

a man in a dark suit who followed them in; and when they moved to the terrace outside for lunch, he came out immediately after them and sat down a few tables away. There he was joined presently by another man in a similar dark suit, the two of them having none of the seaside vacationing air of the other guests, and the two put their heads together and kept looking at her and Ramón as they talked. And though the glimpse she had had upstairs had been far too narrow for positive recognition, she felt utterly certain that the second man was the one who had been watching when she left her room.

She had hesitantly asked Ramón what he thought of them.

'I'd already noticed them,' he said. 'Did you ever see two more obvious detectives?'

She told him about what had happened upstairs.

'It looks very bad,' he said grimly. 'He was not watching you, of course, but watching for me. I am still sure you have nothing to fear. Because you are leaving, they will not believe you are important. But I think you are going just in time.'

'But if they're watching you, it means you've been betrayed.'

'Perhaps not so badly. We do not know who our traitor is – or we should have dealt with him. So we do not know how much he can betray. Perhaps very little. Then the Secret Police would not know enough yet to arrest me; they would only be watching.'

'But then it's only a question of time—'

He nodded, tight-lipped.

'I begin to think that everything may have to be postponed. For a while only, but at least until they are off guard again. And I shall go abroad – then they will be certain that I am not in mischief. I could not be organizing a revolution on the Riviera. Would you like to go there?'

'If you'd promise to meet me there, I'd go.'

'I must think about it,' he had said.

Now, two hours later, he strode to her window and stood gazing out unseeingly, with his hands gripping nervously together behind his back. Finally he said: 'Yes, *querida*, I have decided. When I heard you say on the phone just now that you might go to Europe, I knew it was right. Will you think me a coward if I go?'

'Oh, no, Ramón! I want you to be a hero, but you wouldn't help anyone by throwing your life away.'

He turned to her and kissed her hands.

'Then it is settled. You will drive to New York, as you said, and book a passage on the first good boat. You will take your car for us to drive around, because it is much newer than mine, but of course I will pay the expenses. I shall book myself on a plane in about a week, so that I do not seem in too big a hurry, but I shall be there in France when you land.'

'You don't know what a load you've taken off my mind,' she said; and yet as she said it she felt inexplicably as if something else had been taken from her also.

He glanced at his watch.

'We should have your bags taken to the car before they want to charge you another day for the room,' he said practically. 'We can wait downstairs for your travel agent.'

They went downstairs together with her luggage and watched it stowed in the trunk of her sedan. Venino tipped the bellboys and dismissed them.

Beryl Carrington felt a strange vague uncomfortableness as they faced each other alone again, with nothing to do but to kill time and nothing special to talk about. Nothing, that is, except something most personal. Everything else had been wrapped up so quickly and finally. But right up until then, the kisses he had recently pressed on her hands were the nearest approach to emotion there had been between them. In the beginning she had been charmed and relieved by his correctness. But she had always been convinced that at the proper time, when it could be done without crudity and disrespect, his attentions would become warmer. It could not be any other way, with such a romantic enterprise binding their lives together. Yet now that he could scarcely avoid making some declaration about themselves, she found herself desperately unready to receive it.

He took her hand and drew her towards him.

'You must not worry about me,' he said, and a flutter of pure panic suddenly shook her.

'Why not?' asked the Saint's coolest and most languid voice. 'I'd say there was a whole lot to worry about.'

They turned like two marionettes jerked with the same string.

Beryl Carrington's startlement was at first almost grateful – until her eyes fell on the briefcase that Simon carried, and grew round with blank dismay. But Ramón Venino's face turned yellow with the sickly anaemia of a sceptic who for the first time believes that he is seeing an incontrovertible ghost; and then, as he too saw the briefcase, his eyes literally jolted in their sockets as if he had been hit behind the head. And the Saint strolled closer, around the side of the car which had concealed his silent approach.

'As a one-man revolution,' he remarked, 'I'd say he was a lousy actuarial risk.'

Venino put forth a colossal effort that dragged his congealing stare from the briefcase to Mrs Carrington.

'What is this?' he demanded hoarsely. 'I thought—'

'Yes, I gave it to him,' she said with sudden assurance. 'I was afraid you were gambling too much on the police thinking I wasn't important. And I've told you all about him. He promised he'd get it to Florida for me.'

'And if you insist,' Simon said earnestly, 'I will. I'll even get you a police escort for it.'

As though they had only been waiting to explode that boast,

the two men in dark suits whom Mrs Carrington had temporarily lost sight of materialized from between other parked cars and hurled themselves at the Saint in a co-ordinated rush that had one of them clamped on to each of his arms before Mrs Carrington fully grasped what was happening. But the Saint seemed only inconsequentially put out.

'You're grabbing the wrong guy,' he said, without struggling.

One of the dark-suited men turned to Mrs Carrington.

'This is the man who has been annoying you?' he said.

'Annoying me?' she repeated in complete bewilderment.

'We were called by someone who spoke for you,' explained one of the detectives. 'About some lunatic who has been making telephone calls and trying to force himself into your room. We understood you did not want to complain personally, or to have a scandal, so we have only been watching to catch this man the next time he annoyed you.'

'But no one has been annoying me,' she said helplessly.

'You are Mrs Carrington?'

'Yes.'

'Mrs *Beryl* Carrington?'

'Yes.'

'Somebody must have been playing a joke on you,' said the Saint.

'This gentleman is a friend of mine,' she said shakily. 'Please let him go.'

The two plain-clothes men looked at Venino with a sort of forlorn desperation, and one of them said: '*Usted no sabe nada de esto, señor?*'

With his eyes flickering back to the briefcase which Simon still held, Venino said brusquely, '*Nada*. As the *señor* says, it is either a mistake or a stupid trick.'

The two detectives looked at each other. In unison, they raised their eyebrows, they pursed their lips, they shrugged.

Their vice-like grips unhooked themselves from the Saint's arms. They stepped back, and bowed with a sort of defeated sarcasm.

'Pardon us, Mrs Carrington,' they said, and turned stiffly on their heels.

Beryl Carrington shook her head dazedly.

'I don't understand – any of this—'

'It is a Secret Police trick, if nothing worse,' Venino snapped.

'I think it was your trick, Ramón,' Simon said pleasantly. 'You called the cops in her name and told them that cock-and-bull story to get them to keep a watch on her. Then you pointed the sleuths out to prove that they were watching you. It's just dawned on me that that may have been the clincher that sold her on going to Europe. Did you just decide that this afternoon, Beryl?'

'Yes,' she said with unnatural steadiness. 'It was exactly like that.'

'And maybe that was the only proof you ever had that anyone was after him.'

'It was. But—'

'He is trying to confuse you,' Venino said harshly. 'We must get back that briefcase.'

'This?' Simon held up the alligator bag by the handle, so that the telephone directory slid out into his other hand through the seam he had opened along its under side. 'Or the priceless contents?'

He showed Mrs Carrington the book, making sure that she recognized what it was.

'This,' he said reverently, 'is the God-damnedest Underground you ever saw the secret list of. Every single soul in Greater Havana who can afford a telephone is a member.'

Venino snatched the directory from him.

'You fool,' he snarled. 'If anyone had discovered the marks in invisible ink against each name that is one of us—'

Mrs Carrington was almost shaken out of her wavering, and even the Saint's eyes blinked with reluctant admiration. But he shook his head slowly.

'It's a nice try, Ramón,' he conceded. 'But it won't score. Can you think back coldly and impartially just for a few seconds, Beryl – even though it'll hurt? Do you really believe that any Underground movement that had any hope of getting as far out of the ground as its own tombstone would have a list of members that was as easy as that for anyone to get hold of? Or that anyone who was bright enough to live long enough to become a top man in that sort of conspiracy would tell you all about it after a few rumbas, and place the life of every last member in your hands because of the sympathy he saw in your pretty eyes? I knew he was taking you for a ride the minute you told it to me that way. But I didn't appreciate quite what a ride it was until I checked on this business about the Dictatorship. And that really knocks the underpinnings from under the whole gehoozis. Because there just ain't no such animal.'

'He is not a fool, *querida*,' Venino hissed. 'He is insane.'

'Oh, I suppose it isn't altogether our kind of democracy, Beryl,' Simon said imperturbably. 'But there aren't any downtrodden masses aching to shake off their chains. There may be a revolution some day, but it'll just be one political faction against another, not an uprising of the people. If Ramón hadn't scared the wits out of you, you could have asked some of 'em for yourself. You still can.'

'Are you trying to destroy us all?' Venino asked passionately.

Simon glanced over his shoulder. As he had rather anticipated, the two men in dark suits had withdrawn, but not completely out of the picture. They had retreated to a polite distance out of earshot, but not out of sight.

'We still have a couple of cops handy, Beryl,' he said.

'Would you like me to walk over to them and say 'Nuts to the President!' so you can see if they shoot me?'

'I'm trying,' Mrs Carrington said, 'not to have hysterics.'

'I'm sorry,' said the Saint contritely. 'I'd better leave, before you get mad and call off our deal on the car.'

Mrs Carrington's mouth opened, but no sound came from it. Sound came, however, from Ramón Venino.

'What deal on the car?' he demanded in a cracked voice.

'I made Mrs Carrington an offer to buy it,' Simon said calmly. 'She wants to get something more sporty, like a convertible, and I'm paying a much better price than she could get on a trade-in. I'm taking this one over from her in Miami. I guess she hadn't had time to tell you.'

'But we are taking this car to Europe,' Venino said shakily.

'That's silly,' the Saint scoffed. 'If she wants a flashy sports job, Europe's the place to get one.'

'I will not allow it,' Venino said.

Mrs Carrington looked at him wonderingly.

'Why not?' she asked, and never quite knew why she said it like that.

'It would break my heart. Yes, I am sentimental. Because of this car, we met. In this car, I showed you my home town. In this car, my heart found a new life. Call me a temperamental Latin if you like, but I do not want to see Europe with you in any other car!'

Simon lighted a cigarette, and an immeasurable artistic contentment was ripening within him.

'What he means,' he said, 'is that any other car would not be worth anything like as much to him. Which isn't surprising, because this would probably be the most valuable car in Europe, if not in the whole world. As I have it figured, it should sell for around three hundred thousand dollars any place where there's a fairly open market for gold, which of course rules out the United States. A really fabulous build-up has gone into jockeying you into making that trip with a date to meet Ramón on the other side.'

They were both listening to him now, without interruption and in a weird kind of stillness. And the Saint put one foot up on the rear bumper and leaned a forearm lazily on his knee.

'Big-time thieves aren't an exclusively *yanqui* product. They crop up all over. Down here, I guess Ramón will rank *numero uno*. Anyway, he and his mob knocked off an armoured carload of three hundred grand's worth of gold bars a few weeks before we got here. But they couldn't sell it here, and the problem was to get a heavy load like that out of the country with the cops looking everywhere for it. Ramón's brilliant idea was to watch for a likely female tourist, alone, bringing her own car over. With a simple little accident and a lot of charm, he was able to get away with the car for long enough for his mob to take impressions of suitable parts of it. They cast the gold in the moulds and plated it while he was keeping you on the hook with his personality and his fairy tales, and last night when he had the car again they put on the new gold trimmings.' The knife that had been Pancho's flashed suddenly as Simon thumbed the catch that released the blade. 'For instance, I'll bet that if we carved a notch in this bumper—'

Ramón Venino moved then, his hand going to his hip pocket and coming out with something that he kept mostly hidden under the drape of his coat.

'That is enough,' he said. 'You will both come with me, now, in this car.'

Mrs Carrington gasped as she saw the gun, but the Saint only glanced at it and then over Venino's shoulder.

'You made one mistake when you had your fat friend try to warn me off at the Bambú,' he said. 'You made another when you sent him back with a pal this afternoon to defenestrate me – meaning heave me out of a window. Because I clobbered both of them and sent for the police, but I left before the police got there. So now the police have followed me here, and teamed up with the two that we had already. You'd be making the classic mistake of all time if you shot me now, while they're all standing behind you.'

'You must think me a fool if I would believe that,' Venino sneered.

'I assure you, *compadre*, he tells the truth,' one of the policemen said.

5

'Why did he have to pick on me?' Beryl Carrington said.

'You mean, why couldn't he have put gold bumpers on his own car, and shipped it to Europe?' said the Saint. 'We don't know yet, but I'll bet anything you like on a guilty conscience. Ramón and his mob could never be sure when they might be suspected, so they wanted to plant the loot on someone who would never be suspected.'

'But why me?' she said.

'I guess they just watched the boats from Key West, and you were the first good prospect they saw.'

'It didn't have to be me,' she said in a queer stony voice.

'Did you hear what the gendarmes said about that twenty thousand dollars reward? I think we should split it down the middle.'

'I couldn't care less.'

'You can do a lot of good things with ten thousand bucks.'

'Don't you see?' she said. 'I wish it had never happened. Or if it had to happen, I wish I'd never seen you. I wish I'd never known.'

Simon Templar looked at her shrewdly and with unwonted compassion for a while, and then he stood up.

'This isn't the end of romance,' he said. 'But if you'd gone on with Venino, one day you'd have had to find out, and that might have been the end. Now you think the most wonderful toy you ever had has been broken, and it was all you had. But it isn't all you'll ever have. Don't start to believe that.'

'Please go now,' she said. But as he opened the door she raised her eyes and said, 'But call me tomorrow.'

Simon went out and let the doorman earn a quarter for lifting one finger at a taxi.

'You have plans for tonight, sir?' said the driver, as the cab got under way. 'You should meet a nice Cuban girl. It happens I have a niece, very young, very beautiful . . .'

THE GOLDEN FROG

INTRODUCTION*

For the benefit of readers who may not be familiar with the names of too many scientists, I should like to mention that the Dr Zetek who is mentioned in this story is not a fictitious character, and the yarn should really be dedicated to him. For, while I was in Panama, it was he who arranged for me the rare experience of a visit to Barro Colorado, the island in Gatun Lake which the Smithsonian Institute with the cooperation of the Panamanian Government has been able to preserve as *virgo intacta* for the study of tropical ecology, and where in the mess hall maintained for visiting naturalists I saw a brilliant colour photo and learned description of his equally non-fictitious discovery, *atelopus zeteki*, the golden frog (the real jumping one, that is) which started the Saint on the following adventure.

Leslie Charteris

*From *The Saint Mystery Magazine* (UK), October 1965

I

Professor Humphrey Nestor, it must be revealed *ab initio*, had never actually been a member of the faculty of any of the illustrious colleges whose names he liked to drop casually into his conversation; nor, to be utterly candid, did he possess any of the academic qualifications which could have made it even remotely possible that he might some day be offered such an appointment. In fact, some prejudiced persons had been heard to asseverate, perhaps wishfully, that the only chair of importance that Mr Nestor was ever likely to occupy would be wired for high-voltage electricity; but this was an exaggeration. Mr Nestor was not by nature addicted to violence.

At this time he was only fifty-five, and still spry and lean of frame; but his hair had already attained the snowy whiteness which in the minds of the gullible is simultaneously suggestive of both wisdom and benignity, and he had parlayed that fortunate colouration into a trim moustache and goatee which, combined with the bifocals that had been thrust upon him willy-nilly by the normal incipience of presbyopia, gave him an air of erudite distinction that only the most adamantine sceptic could resist. And though he had no right whatsoever to the title which he had adopted as a vocational convenience, he was by no means illiterate. He owned, among a unique collection of forgeries, an absolutely authentic degree from a minor university whose track team had been well repaid by his youthful gift of running very fast for short distances; and he had a predilection for magazines of the popular science and science-fiction type which gave him not only a useful repertoire of abstrusities but also invaluable models of what the public expected a Professor to be like. As a result, Professor Nestor was a much more convincing Professor than almost any ivied turret could produce – as a great many suckers had expensively learned.

Yet such are the vicissitudes to which a great talent may be subjected that on the day we are talking about Professor Humphrey Nestor was scraping the bottom of the barrel as literally as he was trying to suck the last drops of ice-diluted fluid through the straws that protruded from what had once been an ambrosial beaker of Panamanian rum punch.

'I can't think what we've done to deserve such miserable luck,' he lamented.

'One thing is, you're getting old,' said the shapely blonde who passed as his daughter Alice.

Their real relationship was of course much less conventional; but since she was almost exactly half his age, the father-daughter was far more disarming than if he had introduced her as his wife, and indeed was likely to arouse positive sympathy instead of a raised eyebrow. And there was the added advantage that this arrangement imposed no tiresome restrictions on the exploitation of her sex appeal, which was not negligible.

There were times, however, when he wished she would maintain a semblance of filial respect when they were alone, and this was one of them.

'You're in a rut,' she said, with unsympathetic candour. 'Sure, we had a good line once, but nobody's been buying it lately. Instead of moaning about your bad luck, why don't you start figuring out something new?'

'Because it's still a good line,' said the Professor stubbornly. 'The very best. I spent a lot of time dreaming it up.

It's worked fine for us down here – and we're lucky to be here.'

There was much truth in that.

Some five years earlier, a purely technical error in the use of the mails had occasioned this rather abrupt deflection in a career which had long been devoted (with remarkably few interludes in jail, all things considered) to the cause of parting fools from their money with a promptness that would have gladdened the proverb-coiner's heart. One day Professor Nestor woke up to realize that instead of a civil suit which he could have outranged by simply stepping over the nearest state line, he had laid himself open to federal retribution that would not be halted by any parochial boundaries within the United States. But he was a provident and foresighted man in other respects, and was never without an alternative identity sufficiently well documented to satisfy the liberal requirements of most Latin American countries, which are not inclined to make excessive difficulties for apparently solvent tourists; a banana boat happened to be sailing from New Orleans at a moment which it would be almost an understatement to call opportune, and in due course the Professor and Alice found themselves in Panama with an indefinite period of exile ahead of them.

Humphrey Nestor surveyed the situation and was not displeased. Such a precipitate departure as they had been forced to make might easily have landed them in any of the forsaken backwaters of the hemisphere; instead of which, they had been neatly unloaded on one of the world's busiest bottlenecks. Through the Canal passed endless fleets of passenger-bearing vessels of all sizes and qualities, not to mention the coastwise trade and cruise boats of the Pacific and the Caribbean which touched the ports on either side of the isthmus, providing one of the basic essentials for the exercise of Mr Nestor's peculiar talent: a bountiful supply of transients with time on their hands, money in the bank, a minimum of factual information about the locale, and a romantic predisposition to believe strange and wonderful tales appropriate to an exotic setting. He was reasonably sure that he had left no trail behind him, and he was not much worried about the police of the American zone, who were more concerned with the security of the Canal than with operations of his type. And there was the unique advantage of a completely invisible and unguarded frontier with the Republic of Panama, so that merely by crossing a street one could pass back and forth between jurisdictions – a convenience which he found extraordinarily comforting.

All that remained was to adapt one of their tried and proved routines to get the utmost value out of the scenery and atmosphere at their disposal; and this he had accomplished with such virtuosity that there were now twenty-three thousand dollars in a pension fund which they had accumulated by ruthlessly setting aside fifty per cent of all their killings.

Alice was the sole custodian of this fund, which she had insisted on as her price for continuing the partnership.

'We're not going to live this way for ever,' she said. 'We're going to save up, and one day we're going to retire and live like any other retired people, without ever having to worry again.'

There were times when the Professor wondered whether he was really included in those plans for her future. But he was forced to accept her terms, for very few bunco compositions can be played effectively as solos, and she was an invaluable confederate. This arrangement, however, explains the apparent paradox in the statement made earlier that at this moment the Professor was suffering an acute financial squeeze.

'If we don't find a mark very soon indeed,' he said, 'I'm

going to have to borrow something from our retirement fund.'

'Then you'd better find a mark very soon, Pappy,' she said promptly. 'Because our retirement fund is not lending.'

'But this would be an emergency,' he argued. 'After all, we've both lived off the half share that doesn't go into your fund, and all the other expenses came out of it too. You can't do any good in this racket without capital.'

'Then I hope you connect while you've still got some,' she said. 'But if I let you get your fingers into that fund on one excuse, pretty soon you'd have another, and before long there'd be no more fund, and we'd be on our way to the poor-house in a Cadillac just like when I met you.'

'You haven't done badly since we teamed up,' he reminded her tartly. 'For a B-girl who never did anything bigger on her own than roll a drunk—'

'That's why I went for you, Pappy,' she said sweetly. 'I knew you had what it takes. Only I don't know how I'd feel if I thought you'd lost it.'

'I could do fine if only we got a break,' he said. 'I had that rich Australian solidly hooked last week, didn't I? And then his daughter has to get polio and he turns around and flies home and that's probably the last we'll hear of him.'

'Anyhow, he got away,' she said. 'And we didn't get a cent out of him.'

The Professor sighed over the remorseless inflexibility of feminine logic, and looked glumly around in search of some happier conversational diversion.

They were sitting in the bar of what unschooled tourists will always call, redundantly, 'The' El Panamá – at that time the newest and most luxurious (and most expensive) hotel in the Republic. Built and operated by Americans for Americans, it was the counterpart of fifty kindred air-conditioned caravanserais which had raised their uniformly modernistic façades of glass and concrete and aluminium during that generation amid every conceivable skyline from mud huts to minarets and Spanish tile to Norman towers, all dedicated to the proposition that since air travel had brought the farthest corners of the globe into everybody's back yard, no traveller should be allowed to feel that he had ever left home. Sooner or later an inevitable nine-tenths of the best-heeled travellers were bound to stroll at least once through its patios and lobbies, and Professor Humphrey Nestor was a regular customer for reasons which happily combined business with pleasure.

'As the great Barnum said, there'll be another along in a minute,' he remarked bravely. 'Now suppose we had one more drink—'

'We'll have six more, if you can pay for them,' said Alice accommodatingly. 'Only don't try to stick me with the tab, because you'd look awful undignified trying to race me to the door.'

They might have continued indefinitely with another bout of these genial exchanges, but at that very moment a new patron strolled into the bar whose aspect called a truce to recriminations as abruptly as a soundless bomb.

His supremely comfortable costume of feather-weight slacks, sandals, and a shirt that appeared to have been designed with the help of a kaleidoscope, plus the inevitable camera slung over one shoulder, branded him frankly and cheerfully as a tourist. But not just any tourist. There were graduations in these markings for which the Professor and Alice had eyes that would have sent a vulture looking for an oculist. The slacks were tailored of the lightest Italian shantung, the shirt was a still finer silk, even the sandals were of beautiful leather and finished like expensive shoes. The camera was the newest and most costly model Leica. And his face and arms had the bone-deep kind of tan, subtly different from the superficial browning of a brief vacation, which marks a man who habitually spends most of his time out of doors. True, there are humble labourers who share that privilege with the leisured wealthy, but although this man was slim-waisted and wide-shouldered he moved with a casual grace and assurance that left no possible doubt which category he belonged in. And although an indefinable keenness of eye and rakishness of feature suggested that he might at some time have known a ruggeder form of outdoor life than a golf course or a fashionable beach, a certain spirit of adventure in the victim was a contribution rather than an obstacle to the ideal dénouement of the plot in which the Professor and Alice had so often played their profitable roles. In fact, if they had been given some kind of supernatural carte blanche to design the type of character that they would have most liked to see walk into the bar at that moment, it might well have turned out to be a recognizable facsimile of the newcomer whom we have just described.

For almost half a minute they were too distrustful of this apparently divine dispensation to be able to speak.

It was Mr Nestor who recovered his voice first. The new arrival, he finally convinced himself, was no mirage of the kind which is reported to torment the thirst-crazed wanderer in the Sahara. Mr Nestor could see him quite normally and three-dimensionally through the upper part of his bifocals. And Alice had seen the same thing at the same moment. He could tell by the pure spirituality that had descended on her rather childish face, and by the fact that she had not taken advantage of his own silence to get in any more shrewd licks.

'Well,' he said heavily, at last, 'will you trust me to start this one in my old-fashioned way, or would you rather take over?'

'Go ahead, Pappy,' she said, and added almost affectionately: 'Just don't ham it up too much like you do sometimes.'

He waited with agonizing patience until his quarry's drink

was almost finished, and then he picked up his modest box camera and ambled over to the bar.

'Pardon me, sir,' he said bashfully, 'but I see that you're a photographer, and I wondered if I could impose on you – if you'd be so kind as to snap a picture of my daughter and myself with *our* camera?'

'Why, of course,' Simon Templar said amiably.

'There's no hurry. Whenever you can spare a moment.'

'I've nothing but moments to spare right now.'

Simon laid a dollar bill on the bar and slid off his stool. The Professor turned back towards the table where he had been sitting.

'Alice, dear,' he said, 'the gentleman very kindly says he'll oblige us right away.'

As she came to join them, he said shyly: 'My name is Professor Humphrey Nestor, and this is my daughter Alice. Might I know whom we are indebted to?'

Simon had a preposterous alias which in some circumstances came almost instinctively to his lips.

'Sebastian Tombs,' said the Saint, without hesitation.

2

'It's terribly sweet of you,' Alice said, looking up at him with big blue eyes as if he had volunteered to bring her the moon in a platinum casket. 'You know how it is – usually Pappy takes a picture of me, and then I take a picture of him, but we never have one of the two of us together.'

'I know how it is,' said the Saint sympathetically.

'Really, I should get one of those timer gadgets that let you get into your own pictures,' the Professor reproached himself.

They went out into the glaring shade under the umbrella trees, and the two Nestors stood rather stiffly and naïvely side by side, smiling at the camera, while Simon clicked the shutter.

'We ought to have one with the Frog,' Alice said.

'Yes, yes,' agreed the Professor, frowning. 'If we aren't taking up too much of Mr Tombs's time . . .'

'Not at all,' said the Saint agreeably.

It would have been almost a psychological impossibility for anyone with a shred of human curiosity to have torn himself away without waiting to see that last shot.

Alice opened her capacious purse and took from it a soft leather pouch with a drawstring. From the pouch she took a package wrapped in tissue, about the size of an orange. The Professor fussed around helping her to unwrap it, until the contents was revealed on a nest of loosened paper.

It actually was a frog. A rather slender, long-bodied frog. Or to be more accurate, a carving or moulding of a frog, very simply but excellently done. And the most startling thing was that it looked as if it might have been made of pure gold.

'Could you come a little closer,' said the Professor, 'and get a good picture of the frog, perhaps with just our faces looking at it?'

Simon moved on obligingly, while they held the frog up on its wrapping between them, and clicked the shutter again.

'Hold it a moment,' he said, unslinging his Leica. 'I'd like to get one for myself, for a souvenir.'

They held still briefly while he took the picture again, and then quickly helped each other to re-wrap the figurine.

'We're very, very grateful,' said the Professor, with unsophisticated earnestness.

'We took Mr Tombs away from a nice cool drink,' Alice said. 'I think we ought to get him another.'

'Of course – how stupid of me! Won't you let us do that, Mr Tombs?'

'I was hoping you'd say that,' Simon replied, with a beatifically disarming smile which made it seem unthinkable that he could actually have meant it.

They went back into the cool dimness of the bar, and a round of Panamanian punches was ordered. After which there was a kind of conversational hiatus, as if in spite of his sincerity and good intentions the Professor's social gifts had been exhausted by the providing of refreshment. He seemed to withdraw into an unworldly introspection; and his daughter only seemed to be able to look at him devotedly and rather anxiously, as if she knew what was on his mind and would have liked to help him with it but did not know how to.

It was obviously up to the Saint to break this awkward pause, and it would have taken a positive effort to refuse the handiest and most natural gambit.

'That frog of yours,' he remarked. 'That's quite an unusual piece.'

'It is,' said the Professor, coming a few miles closer in interstellar space.

'Not that it's any of my business, but it almost looked as if it was made of gold.'

'It is.'

'Pappy,' Alice said gently, 'aren't you being a little rude? I can see why Mr Tombs would be curious. After all, we made him take our pictures with it.'

'Yes, so we did. Pray accept my apologies, Mr Tombs,' said the Professor contritely. 'I was only afraid of boring you. You couldn't really care about our scientific troubles.'

'Never mind our scientific troubles,' Alice said. 'Tell him the interesting part.'

Mr Nestor pursed his lips.

'Well,' he ventured diffidently, 'did you ever hear of *Atelopus zeteki*?'

'Do you catch it on a rod and line,' Simon asked, 'or from going barefoot in hotel bathrooms?'

'It's the Golden Frog of Panama,' Alice explained.

The Professor dredged an inner pocket of his sagging seersucker and came out with an ancient and shabby wallet of portfolio dimensions. He fumbled, blinking nervously, through an assortment of beat-up snapshots, newspaper clippings, old envelopes and tattered palimpsests on all kinds of paper, which bulked it to the thickness of a light novel, and extracted a documentary relic which on being gingerly unfolded proved to be a page from an old issue of *Life*. It carried a single photograph in full colour which centred on a large tropical leaf on which was crouched a long-bodied frog that was almost entirely a bright yellow from nose to toe.

'That's the Golden Frog,' said the Professor. 'It's one of Nature's oddities, which could only have evolved in the tropical rain forest around here. A beautiful creature, isn't it? You'll notice that that one has a certain mottling of black on it. Some of them have polka dots. The ones that are all gold are quite rare. But it's such a fragile product of its environment that just a few minutes' exposure to ordinary sunlight are enough to kill it!'

He was simply paraphrasing, quite accurately, the caption under the picture, but he had a way of doing it so authoritatively that he made it sound more as if the caption was quoting him. Letting the dupe handle and read that indisputably genuine page of *Life* at the same time was a trick that invariably clinched the acceptance of his own scientific standing, and even more subtly it extended an aura of veracity over the fable that he had to pyramid on that one fact.

'That's very interesting,' said the Saint respectfully. 'Did you discover it?'

'Oh, no. It was discovered by a former colleague of mine, Dr Zetek. That's why it carries his name. What I discovered was the frog that you saw – what we might call *Atelopus nestori.*'

Professor Nestor chuckled coyly over his scholarly little joke.

'Of course, our golden frog was modelled from the real one,' Alice said.

'You can easily see how it would happen,' said the Professor. 'Long before Dr Zetek or any of us came here, the real golden frog was naturally known to the aborigines. And it was the sort of phenomenon which could hardly help striking the imagination of a primitive and superstitious people. The transformation of a tadpole into a frog of any kind is almost like seeing a miracle of evolution take place under your very eyes. Then think how still more awed they must have been when they saw that some tadpoles apparently no different from the others turned into frogs that seemed to be made out of the same precious metal that they would find in rare nuggets among the gravel of their river beds. Add to that the peculiarity that these frogs were so delicate that if captured, no matter how gently they were handled, they would die for no reason that a savage could understand – and to anyone who knows anything about primitive psychology, you have all the necessary ingredients for the origination of a religious cult.'

'You mean your golden frog is a museum piece?'

'Well, at least five hundred years old. Perhaps a great deal more. The only other one that I had ever seen – before I came here – was brought to me when I was lecturing on pre-Columbian artefacts at Michigan State University, by a tourist who picked it up on the San Blas Islands. He wanted to know if it had any antique value apart from the metal in it. Of course, I recognized at once that it was not San Blas workmanship, but he could tell me no more about its history. Naturally it hadn't occurred to him to ask the Indian who sold it to him how he had come by it. I could only tell, from certain technical indications, that it was very old, perhaps even contemporary with the Mayan culture. I tried to buy it, but the owner was much too wealthy: the cash value meant nothing to him, but he wanted it as a souvenir, and an antique to boast about as well if he could have obtained an official pedigree for it.'

'But you don't give up so easily, do you, Pappy?' said Alice adoringly.

'I must say, I went on thinking about it. And then, quite by chance, I happened to hear of Dr Zetek's golden frogs. One glance at a picture was enough to show me that they must have been the model for the little metal frog that I had been shown. After that, to a scientific mind with my special background, the other deductions were almost elementary. Some prehistoric culture in Panama must have made a fetish of the golden frog and used images of it in their rites . . . But I must be boring you.'

'Not in the least,' said the Saint truthfully. 'This is something they don't have in the guide books.'

The Professor nodded complacently.

'Not yet. I was not foolish enough to discuss my deductions with anyone at that point – except Alice.'

'You wouldn't believe how careful a scientist has to be these days,' Alice explained. 'It's almost as bad as being an inventor. There's so much competition for the only college jobs that pay a living wage, and so many colleges seem to hire professors just for their box-office value, according to the books they've written and the things they're supposed to have discovered – so when a professor thinks he's on the track of something really big he has to guard it like an atomic bomb so that somebody else won't steal it.'

'You can't blame them, considering how few decent salaries a university can pay, except to a football coach,' said the Professor, with an unworldly resignation that would have tweaked the heartstrings of the most indurated cynic. 'Let's just say that I had enough human vanity to hope that my own name might go down to history along with some discovery that I'd made all by myself. I had a little money that I'd saved up to give Alice a start in life, but she insisted we should spend it on this. Finally I took my sabbatical, and we came down here to try to find the evidence of this cult. We made three different expeditions, into parts of the country that had never been explored. Some of it was really rough – especially for Alice.'

He paused to glance admiringly at his daughter, and Simon followed the glance with a raised eyebrow.

'Did you go along too?'

'I wouldn't have missed it for the world,' Alice said. 'Even when I was a little girl I was always pestering the boys to take me hunting and fishing with them. I only wish I could live like that all the time.'

This was one of Mr Nestor's deadliest inspirations. He had found that the time-honoured bait value of a blue-eyed blonde with the face and the figure of a Hollywood starlet was multiplied ten-fold by the revelation that she would honestly prefer a fishing camp to a night club. In the presence of such devastating credentials, strong men became misty-eyed and indeed were sometimes hard to bring back to mundane preoccupations. Mr Nestor observed an unmistakable hint of reverence in the way Mr Tombs was looking at Alice, and hurried on before he lost his audience completely.

'I won't bore you with all the details. But we succeeded – more than I'd even dared to hope. We not only found proof of the cult of the Golden Frog, we found perhaps *all* the relics of it that will ever be found.'

Simon removed his gaze from Alice with undisguised reluctance.

'You mean you found more than that one frog I took a picture of?'

'To be exact, we found thirty-seven. And we found them all at once, in a cave that we literally stumbled into by the sheerest accident.'

'Some defunct witch-doctor's Olde Frogge Shoppe?'

'I think there's a better explanation. As you'll remember, the Spanish conquistadors were here, as they were all over Central and South America. And as you know, the main thing the Spaniards were looking for was gold. It can't have taken the priests of the Frog very long to find that out, but they must have been smarter than most of the other Indian tribes. They must have rounded up as many of the images as they could and hidden them in this cave – the entrance was so well hidden that no one could ever have found it unless he accidentally fell into it like I did. The specimen that the tourist brought to me must have been one that some individual hid on his own or that got lost somewhere, but the main collection was never found. Probably all the priests who knew where it was died under the tortures of the Inquisition without betraying the secret. Anyhow, no one can have set eyes on their treasure again until we found it.'

'Are the other frogs all the same size?'

'More or less, most of them. My hypothesis is that they were in the nature of icons, issued to minor priests or chieftains as a symbol of authority. But there were three images as big as footballs which must have presided over important lodges or perhaps their equivalent of cathedrals, and one absolute whopper, nearly as big as Alice, which must have been the original idol that all the others were modelled from.'

The Saint's lips took the shape of an awed whistle.

'You don't say they were solid gold?'

'I have seen no evidence that those Indians knew the arts of plating, or making alloys,' answered the Professor dryly.

'And to think I once started to feel sorry for you,' said the Saint. 'I should apologize. If I'd known an archaeologist could hit that kind of pay dirt, I might have gone in for it myself.'

The Professor smiled faintly.

'Would it be impertinent to ask what your business is, Mr Tombs?'

'I suppose you'd have to call me a speculator,' said the Saint with studious honesty. 'I dabble in anything that looks interesting at the time. I may say I've done pretty well at playing my hunches.'

If there could be any more mouth-watering description of the type that Professor Nestor prayed every night that Providence would send him on the morrow, the Professor had yet to hear it. Only a lifetime of professional discipline enabled him to sigh with the convincing tinge of envy that was called for at this point.

'I wish I could say the same, Mr Tombs. I suppose I just wasn't born under a lucky star.'

'With a cave full of golden idols, you've certainly got problems. Like income tax, I suppose.'

'But the idols are still there in the cave, Mr Tombs.'

'Till you go back for them.'

'Yes, yes. That, of course, is the problem.'

'And we don't want to lose our heads over it,' Alice said.

Simon frowned interrogatively.

'We'd just about taken it all in,' elaborated the Professor, 'and we were heading back to camp for the cameras and flash bulbs to make a proper record before we disturbed anything, when the headhunters attacked. It would be hard for you to believe, Mr Tombs, sitting here; but in less than an hour's flying time you could parachute into a jungle world as untamed as it was before Columbus sailed ... We'd been hearing the drums for days, but hoped they were only trying to scare us. It was a tragic underestimate. The native bearers we'd left in camp never had a chance, poor devils, but the uproar told us what had happened. We managed to cut across the river and push off in one of he canoes before we were spotted. We fought a rearguard action downstream for two days before they gave up the chase.'

'Just you and Alice?' Simon asked, open-mouthed.

'And Loro, our half-caste guide and interpreter. A wonderful fellow. I only hope nothing happens to him before we go back. That is,' said the Professor, coming hollowly back to earth, 'if we ever do go back.'

'If I knew where there was a cave full of golden idols,' said the Saint, 'I'd like to see any drum-beating headhunters stop me.'

'Probably you can afford to say that,' Alice said gently. 'But it costs a lot of money to organize the only kind of expedition that'd stand a chance. We're going back to try to raise the money, of course—'

'That shouldn't be difficult.'

'I hope you're right,' said the Professor dubiously. 'But as I told you, you remember, we didn't even get any pictures. We haven't anything to show except the one golden frog that you saw. It all depends on how much my scientific reputation is worth. Well, time will tell.'

'They've got to believe you, Pappy,' Alice said.

'Yes, indeed, my dear.' The Professor patted her hand. He had put on one of his most polished performances, not hamming it any more than the part called for, and if the audience wasn't well hooked he should start learning his business all over again. Now it was up to her to carry the ball. 'But we've bored Mr Tombs enough with our problems.' He consulted his watch. 'And I have to call the curator of the Museum. Will you excuse me?'

He got up and pottered vaguely out into the lobby. He had practised that gait until it had become almost a part of him – it suggested a kind of ingenuous and earnest helplessness which was peculiarly convincing. Alices' eyes followed him protectively.

'Poor darling,' she said. 'It means so much to him.'

Simon offered her a cigarette.

'There's no real chance that you won't raise the money is there? I should think he'd only have to wire his University—'

'It isn't as easy as that. You see, no one even heard of the Frog cult before he deduced that it must have existed. And you've no idea how sceptical scientists can be, especially about someone else's discovery. It's not only scientists, either. There's a man who has a desk out in the lobby who calls himself Jungle Jim: he organizes jungle trips for tourists. If you asked him, he'd tell you there aren't any headhunters in Panama. Of course he doesn't take his parties anywhere near the headhunter country, and he doesn't want them scared off, but you can imagine what someone who was checking up on our story might think.'

Simon nodded.

'Have you tried already and been turned down?'

'No. As a matter of fact, we've hardly told anyone. We have to be awfully careful. If the Panamanian government heard about it and believed it, they'd claim it and send a company of soldiers to get it. That wouldn't matter to Pappy, so long as he got the scientific credit, but you can guess how many of the frogs would mysteriously disappear on the way back. In fact, the expedition would be just as likely to come back and swear they hadn't found anything at all – or maybe never even come back, if you see what I mean.'

The Saint decided that it was not up to him to dispute this libellous estimate of the Panamanian militia.

'How much would it cost to go in and get those frogs?' he asked.

She had the figure ready arrived at by an intuition that had seldom failed her: it had to be small enough, compared with her assessment of his means, for him to consider without undue anxiety, but it should also encompass every last dollar that the operation might be good for.

'About ten thousand dollars,' she said, and he didn't blink.

'Someone might go for that as a straight business gamble, in return for a fair share of the loot.'

It was not so much a statement as the thinly veiled basis for an offer; but she shook her head.

'That's the trouble. Pappy would never allow it to be treated as loot. All those frogs would have to go into museums. He'd rather they stayed lost for ever than see any of them melted down, or even put up for sale.'

'Then you certainly are looking for a philanthropist.'

'I know, it isn't realistic. But who could mistake my Pappy for a realist? Now, I'm different. If I could get him just a few of those frogs – enough to make one museum exhibit and a lot of pictures, and prove his theory and make him famous – I wouldn't care what happened to the rest.'

Simon regarded her contemplatively, and suddenly she leaned closer and impulsively put a hand on his arm.

'Tell me something,' she said. 'I don't know why I'm talking to you like this, except that I feel you're a terribly wise person. But I've got to ask you. Suppose I managed to find some businessman who was a bit of a gambler, and made a deal with him on my own.' It was consummate artlessness that continued to keep the discussion impersonal, so that she was absolved of any suspicion of propositioning him. 'If I got just a few of those golden frogs for Pappy, he needn't even know what happened to the rest, the headhunters might have found the cave after we left and taken most of them away, but what he didn't know wouldn't hurt him. He could write his articles and be famous and die happy. Would you think I'd done something very wrong or very good?'

Simon pondered for long enough to calculate what the approximate value of the golden frogs that Nestor had described would be.

'I'd think you should have a medal,' he said. 'And if you decide to make anyone that sort of offer, I wish you'd give me the first chance.'

She looked at him in a dazed and startled way as if a halo had literally appeared over his head like a neon light, and her big eyes swam with soft half-unbelieving tears.

'I'm afraid I shall have to desert you tonight, dear,' said Professor Humphrey Nestor, noting the artistic symptoms with approval as he returned to the table. 'Some former colleagues of mine from Columbia are passing through here – they happened to be calling on the curator when I telephoned, so I had to speak to them. They insisted on me joining them for dinner, but I shall not inflict that ordeal on you. I know our shop talk would bore you to death.'

'That's all right,' Alice said, with her eyes still on the Saint and the most tentative conspiratorial smile touching her lips. 'Mr Tombs just asked me if I could get away to have dinner with him.'

3

She suggested the Jardin El Rancho, and as soon as he saw it he had to approve of her selection. It was like the courtyard of a Spanish hacienda, tile-roofed around three sides but uncovered to the stars in the centre, and open everywhere to the perfect mildness of the night. The service was competently unobtrusive, and the lighting was artistic enough to encourage romance without causing eyestrain. But at first they were strictly practical.

'How would you work this scheme of yours?' he asked.

'Remember, I was at the cave too. I know where it is as well as Pappy.'

'You mean you'd go back there yourself – head-hunters and all?'

'I would if I had to,' she said bravely.

He shook his head.

'That doesn't sound so good.'

'I can't say I'm crazy about it,' she admitted. 'So I don't mind telling you I had another idea.'

'Give.'

'Loro – the native guide who took us into that district.'

'Don't tell me he'd want to go back there.'

'He might. He just about adopted Pappy as his own father, but for some weird reason he practically worships me. Probably because I'm blonde and blue-eyed, and I treated him like a human being – oh, yes, and he got an infected foot once, and I fixed him up from the first-aid kit. It sounds ridiculous, but these natives are like children, and he's at least fifteen-sixteenths Indian. And after the headhunters had chased us out, he told us we'd gone about it all wrong, and if he'd known what we were after he could have gone there alone and got it without any trouble.'

Simon tenderly impaled a pink shrimp on his fork, coated it lightly with sauce, and slid it between his teeth to confirm an earlier impression that the shrimps of Panama are for some unexplored reason the most crisply ambrosial representatives of their genus in all the legendary seven seas.

'Do you know where to find this reckless warrior?'

'Yes, he's still around as a matter of fact, he came to our hotel a little while before you picked me up – Pappy had already left to meet his friends. He wanted to know if there was any chance of our making another expedition. I was just going to tell him that it wouldn't be for a long time, if ever, because we'd spent all our money; and then I had this idea. I asked him to stop by here at nine o'clock, so you could meet him anyway.'

They had *sancocho*, the rich chicken soup with vegetables that can easily become a meal in itself, but left themselves room for some excellent beef tenderloin sliced in mushroom sauce which was entirely European in conception and flavour. He asked many more details about the finding of the cave of golden frogs and the escape from the headhunters which Professor Nestor had skipped over; but that also had been anticipated. The Professor had read many helpful books, and had schooled her so exhaustively that she was never at a loss. Simon's admiration increased undisguisedly as the meal progressed.

'You'll find campus life pretty tame after this, won't you?' he remarked.

'Oh, I won't be going back there with him. I'd hate to be a burden like that to him, poor dear, on his salary. I earn my own living – I'm a very good secretary. Of course I'll have to look for a new job – I had to give up my old one when we came down here. But now I've developed a yen to see more of the world. I'm going to look for a businessman who does a lot of travelling and who'd like to take a Girl Friday with him.'

'It mightn't be easy to keep him at a strictly business-like distance.'

'Well, that mightn't be hard to take if I really liked him,' she said frankly. 'I'm not hopelessly old-fashioned.'

It was obvious that they could have made beautiful music together.

Loro arrived when they were having coffee, and accepted a seat and a bottle of Balboa beer. He was a pudgy brown man in a clean but unpressed white shirt and trousers, with long black hair, a single gold earring, and a wide white-toothed grin. He looked like a genial brigand, which was precisely what he was. Quite early in the Professor's exile, he had volunteered to carry the Professor's bag from a taxi into a hotel; turning from paying off the driver, the Professor had just been fortunate enough to catch a glimpse of his suitcase and Loro disappearing around the next corner. Mr Nestor, who could still put forth a most respectable turn of speed in an emergency, had overtaken him within two blocks; but to Loro's even greater astonishment he had not capped his victory by calling for the police. Instead, he had given him five dollars and invited him to have a drink. Mr Nestor had already realized that a native accomplice might be almost indispensable to whatever bunco routine he finally adapted to the locale, and the problem of finding a native with the requisite guarantees of unscrupulousness had been most happily solved.

Loro's larcenous instinct immediately recognized a master, and he had become a very gratifying pupil. His part was relatively simple, and he brought to it an innate flair for dramatic deceit.

'I go back any time, *señor*,' he said in response to Alice's prompting. 'Bring back frogs. Me *indio*. No trouble.'

'Then why did they have trouble before, when you were with them?' Simon asked.

'Headhunters seen me with *yanquis*, they think me like *yanqui*. Much trouble. Cut off all heads.' Loro made a graphic gesture, laughing delightedly. '*Yanqui* heads very valuable, but they take mine for small-change. Okeh. Me go alone, wear no clothes, they see me *indio*. Can be friends. No trouble.'

'Why didn't you go back by yourself, then, and get the frogs?'

'Cost much money, *señor*. Too much for me.'

'But I thought they were going to be your friends.'

'Sure. All good friends. Okeh. Me go to cave. Okeh. Me take out frogs. Headhunters see. They know gold very valuable. No more friends.'

'Tell him how you thought of doing it, Loro,' Alice said.

The guide leaned over his bare forearms on the table.

'Take plenty guns, yes. But who going to shoot them? No good take soldiers, they steal everything. Take other *indios*, they no can shoot straight. Or head-hunters come, they run away. Okeh. I got better idea.'

'What is it?'

'Sell guns to headhunters. For gold frogs.'

'Do you think they'd trade?'

'Sure. Headhunters want guns. Get more heads, more quick.' Loro chortled tolerantly. 'Not our heads, we no worry.'

'How many guns would it take?' Simon asked.

'I think, fifty, with bullets – can do.'

'But that's impossible,' Alice said. 'You couldn't bring in that many guns – the Panamanians would think you were trying to start a revolution. And you couldn't buy that many here, for the same reason. Why, we had the worst time getting permits for our .22 and one shotgun.'

'Give me money, I get,' Loro said. 'I have friends keep guns, wait for revolution, wait too long, get tired. They take money for guns now, think maybe they buy more guns *mañana*. But it cost plenty. Maybe two hundred dollars each gun and bullets.'

'Then we wouldn't save anything,' said Alice. 'It would still cost ten thousand dollars.'

'Save much trouble. No fighting. Save heads.'

Simon lighted a cigarette.

'What would you want for doing this?' he asked.

Loro's fat cheeks dimpled on each side of his jolly bandit's smile.

'Me, for love, *señor*. For the *señorita* I love. But perhaps I buy some guns more cheap, not pay all two hundred dollars. Me keep some dollars for working. You will not ask me give back, okeh?'

'Okay,' said the Saint steadily.

Loro stood up, beaming. He bowed deeply to the girl.

'I go now. I tell you soon, all is ready. *Buenas noches, diosa.*'

He was gone, melting into the darkness of the parking lot outside the patio as he might have melted into the jungle. Professor Nestor had painstakingly taught him to do this instead of scooting out as if he had dropped a fire-cracker with a short fuse.

Alice was looking at the Saint with misty eyes.

'I can hardly believe that my crazy idea is coming true,' she said.

'I wouldn't call it so crazy,' he said. 'And I like Loro's contribution. Now that we're more or less partners, would you risk telling me what part of the country this cache of golden frogs is in? I bought a map this afternoon to help my feeble geography.'

He took the map from his pocket and spread it on the table between them. She moved her chair around towards him until their shoulders touched, and the perfume of her hair was sweetly close to his nostrils as she leaned over to study the tinted outlines.

'We're here.' She pointed to the south-eastern end of the Canal. 'We'd have to charter a boat – the same one that Pappy and I had, if we can get it. We go out here, past Taboga Island, and down the coast to the mouth of this river. Then we go up the river – it's quite deep, most of the time, and Loro knows all the channels – up – up around here . . .' Her red lacquered fingernail traced the winding course of the stream more hesitantly, but finally settled on a definite point. 'Yes, the head-hunters' territory starts here, at this third fork. So the cave would be a little farther north, about – there.'

Simon gazed at the map as if instead of its green ink he were seeing the lush rain jungle itself. Even though he was far more familiar with such stories than most men, he felt the tug of romance in it as appreciatively as the most frustrated slave to a stock market report. There could have been no higher tribute to the cunning with which Mr Nestor had blended its ingredients.

'I'm going to enjoy this trip,' he said.

'Would you want to go along?'

She asked the question for necessary information, but he stared at her almost indignantly.

'Do I look like a guy who'd miss anything like that?'

'No – quite the contrary. That's one thing that bothers me. You've got that daredevil look. So I'll have to make a condition. You've got to promise me you won't try to go beyond that third fork on the river. You're not an Indian like Loro, and you couldn't pretend to be. I don't want your head cut off and shrunk and dried. I wouldn't want anything at that price. Promise you won't try to go all the way – or it's no deal.'

It was a classic touch. She acknowledged and openly

hero-worshipped every valiant quality and impulse that a man would like to be credited with, and in the next breath she absolved him of any uncomfortable risk of having to live up to them, and prettily made it a command. Nobody but the Saint would have been so sincerely ungrateful.

'You're the boss,' he said curtly, for there was no doubt that she meant it. 'But we go as far as dam-*yanquis* can. Right?'

'Right.'

'Okeh. But how are you going to explain this to Pappy?'

'You know, we've got reservations to fly back tomorrow night. This has all been so sudden ... The only thing I can think of is that I'll have to make some excuse and let him go alone. But what excuse is there? I can't pretend to be sick, or he'd never go.' She was almost suddenly panic-stricken, groping desperately for an answer. 'I've told him before about wishing I could be a travelling secretary. Could I tell him that you've offered me a job? Would you mind if I did that?'

Simon laughed.

'If it's as easy as that, consider yourself hired.'

She clung to his arm impulsively for a moment.

'If Loro can do what he says he can, I wouldn't hold you to it.'

'I might like being held,' he said. 'But we'll have plenty of time to talk about that. If your father goes for it. I'll just have to keep my fingers crossed, because I won't even be able to help you sell it.'

'Why?'

'I have to go over to Cristobal first thing in the morning. I've got an old friend in the Navy who's stationed on that side, and he promised to show me some sensational tarpon fishing on the Chagres River. He can only get two days off, so I'll be back on Friday. If I find you've checked out, I'll know it was just one of those things.'

'I'll be here, I promise,' she said. 'And by then Loro should have lined up those guns.'

When he left her at her hotel several hours later (Professor Nestor did not make his residential headquarters at El Panamá, both for reasons of economy and because it would have been grossly out of character) she kissed him goodnight, not alarmingly, but with a spontaneous warmth which suggested that her full gratitude would be more than perfunctorily enjoyable.

The Professor was sitting up in bed, wearing a suit of gaudy pyjamas and reading a luridly jacketed paperback.

'We're cooking, Pappy,' she said. 'Everything went just like the script. Even better – he's going away for a couple of days' fishing, so there won't be any problem about seeing you off.'

'Splendid,' said the Professor. 'But I'd better go up to Santa Clara as usual until after he's left, so there'll be no chance of accidentally running into him.'

Santa Clara is a seaside resort on the Pacific coast which is supported mainly by Service personnel and Canal employees, and the average tourist is unlikely even to hear of it, let alone visit it. The Professor had found it a convenient and pleasant place to lie low in when he was supposed to have flown back to the States.

'This'll be one of the long jobs,' Alice said. 'He's determined to go up the river himself as far as I'll let him. That means I'll have to get my hands all fishy and my shoulder sore from that blasted shotgun, and pretend I like it.'

'That's too bad.'

'Oh well, maybe I can get his mind on to something else at least part of the time.'

'I notice your lipstick is a little smudged,' he remarked. 'With a routine as good as we've got, I don't think you need to develop your part so far in that direction as you've been doing.'

'Would you rather get someone else to do it?' she inquired. 'I'll play it the way I feel it, or quit. There isn't much fun for me in this goddamn place. And this is one john who isn't a bit hard to take.'

When the following Friday morning went by without any phone call, she experienced a qualm that was almost as much personal as it was mercenary. She would have sworn that it was practically a toss-up whether Sebastian Tombs was more attracted by herself or the golden frogs, but as the afternoon wore on she began to wonder how both lures could have failed simultaneously. When her phone rang at last, after five o'clock, she was so relieved to hear his voice that her tone was quite angry.

'Whatever happened to you?'

'I've been busy,' he said mildly. 'You sound almost like a wife – or a boss.'

'I'm sorry.' She recovered herself quickly. 'I guess I was getting worried. After seeing my father off and waiting here, I was starting to think how silly I'd look if you never came back.'

'Two things I never stand up, darling,' he said, 'are a beautiful blonde and a chance to make easy money. How's Loro doing?'

'He's been calling me every hour. He's got all the guns and ammunition, but his friends are pressing him for the money.'

'Tell him they can have it as soon as the banks open tomorrow.'

'What have you been so busy with – boss?'

'I got a tip over on the other side that should be worth a fortune,' he said. 'I'll tell you when I see you. Will you be gorgeous and hungry if I pick you up, let's say at seven?'

She had to struggle with an assortment of vague apprehensions until she met him. There were several facts that he might have heard or learned from someone who really knew the country that could have shaken the foundations of his belief in the Professor's imaginative story, yet he had not sounded at all hesitant or sceptical. And when he greeted her he was unrestrainedly jubilant.

'This could be the greatest break for us,' he said. 'My pal on the other side is a fly boy in the Navy, a full Commander, no less, but he's never given up hope of getting rich some day. He thinks he has all the opportunities, and all he needs is a bit of luck. He used to dream about making a forced landing on some unheard-of mountain of gold or a dry wash full of diamonds. Lately it's uranium, and he never takes off without a small Geiger counter in one of his life raft ration cans. Well, every place he goes, he studies up on the local mining laws, because when he strikes pay dirt he doesn't intend to be hornswoggled out of it on some technicality. So I told him that I was thinking of scouting for some gold around here myself – without giving away any of your secrets, of course – and he told me that any minerals you find in Panama belong to the Government, unless you've bought a prospecting concession in advance for the exact area where you find 'em. Did you know that?'

'No,' she said with a blankness that did not have to be feigned.

'Anyway, that's how it is. But my pal knew all the rules, so as soon as I got back here this morning I went to work to take out a prospecting concession on the area you'd shown me on the map. My trouble was, it's such a little-known law that half the officials I talked to hadn't heard of it themselves. Or maybe it's just been too long since anyone did any serious prospecting around here. It took me half the day to find the right bureaucrat who could issue the concession, and it was even tougher getting him to do it on the spot, instead of *mañana*, or next month. But I finally made it. Look!'

He triumphantly unfolded a closely typewritten sheet of

heavy paper. It was trimmed and embellished with an impos-
ing variety of stamps, embossings, ribbons, and sealing-wax,
with a number of ornate signatures, but it was all written in
Spanish, and about the only words that she recognized were
the name of Sebastian Tombs.

'What does it say?'

'Cutting out all the gobbledegook, and the Castilian
whereases and heretofores, it simply says that I have this
prospecting concession for the district you showed me, for
ten days starting tomorrow. You see, to try and prevent
anyone hogging a concession and doing nothing about it,
they put the hell of a price on them, a hundred dollars a day,
and the longest you can take 'em for is three months. Then, if
you make a strike, you can renew 'em by the year; but then
naturally you don't mind the price. That's why the area we're
interested in wasn't tied up: nobody would pay that much
rent for a prospecting licence except for the time he'd be
using it. This fancy scroll cost me a thousand bucks – from
what you told me, I figured ten days should be plenty. But it
gives us the right to keep all the golden frogs we can find in
that time.'

The release from all her apprehensions was such a let-
down that she felt slightly hysterical. It took a titanic effort at
that moment to gaze at him with the awed and eager appre-
ciation which she knew was called for, but somehow she
achieved it.

'You're wonderful,' she said. 'I can see now why you must
be a very successful speculator. You don't miss anything. But
we shouldn't need anything like ten days. I've already
arranged for the boat, and we could leave tomorrow morning
if you like.'

'I like,' said the Saint.

4

The departure of Loro on his intrepid mission to contact the headhunters was in itself almost worth the price of admission. Stripped down to a leopard-skin breechclout, his hair bound in a fillet of brocade that supported a couple of brightly hued parrot feathers, with slashes and curlicues of paint on his face and chest, he would have satisfied any Hollywood studio wardrobe department.

Professor Nestor had had to work hard to persuade Loro that it was necessary to go to these theatrical extremes. It had been comparatively easy to convince him that when the sucker paid over his money, Loro should not simply disappear with all of it, for Loro could never hope to steal that kind of money again on his own, but by working loyally with the Professor and Alice he could expect to share in such killings at frequent intervals for an unlimited future. So, having shown the Saint a stack of oilcloth-wrapped bundles piled in one of the cabins of the boat, with Alice vouching that she had personally inspected and helped to wrap the guns, and having received a thick wad of hundred-dollar bills as promised, he had taken it docilely to the hired car in which Professor Nestor was waiting to leave for Santa Clara, receiving in return only $3,000 for himself and $3,500 in an envelope to be taken back to Alice.

But after the first of such divisions, Loro had taken it for granted that they would all three disappear. The Professor had explained that the victim would then complain to the police, which would be a severe handicap to any future activities. In that case, Loro had suggested cheerfully, it would perhaps be better to take the boat some distance out into the Gulf of Panama, tie the victim to some of the weighted bundles, and drop him over the side. The Professor had explained patiently that the mysterious disappearance of an American, especially a wealthy one, could hardly fail to cause an investigation which would be very likely to come embarrassingly close to them.

'The very best confidence jobs, my dear Loro,' the Professor had pontificated, 'don't even let the sucker know that he's been taken. Isn't it worth a little time and trouble to give our customers a real show for their money, and know that we'll never have to worry about them hollering for the cops?'

He had eventually secured Loro's co-operation, but had reason to doubt if he would ever completely make his point.

Even on this occasion, at the first opportunity Loro had, when the Saint was at the other end of the boat, he said to Alice: 'All this waste plenty time. Much better tonight I—'

He drew an expressive forefinger across his throat. He was half serious and half teasing her, she could tell from his malicious grin, but she was surprised to feel herself shudder.

'Stop it, Loro . . . ! Anyway,' she said, in an attempt to cover up the sharpness of her reaction, 'this one is a perfect example of what we've tried to explain to you. He's actually taken out a prospecting licence from the Government, and he must have told a dozen people where he's going. If he disappeared, we'd have too many tough questions to answer.'

It was only after she had said it that the fantastic thought crossed her mind that Sebastian Tombs might have done all that, and taken pains to tell her about it, as an elaborate precaution against the very thing that Loro was advocating, and a subtle warning that if perchance that was what they had in mind they had better forget it. But the implications that followed were so farfetched that she had made herself brush the idea aside.

Now bundles of alleged rifles and ammunition had been unloaded from the boat and cached at the edge of the jungle, and Loro was ready to play out the last sequence of Professor Nestor's ingenious script.

'You go back down river a little,' he said. 'One mile, plenty, only so headhunters no see. *Mañana*, this time, you come back, you find me with gold frogs.'

'Be careful, Loro,' Alice said anxiously.

'Me always careful,' Loro said, with his jolly bandit's grin. 'No worry. *Hasta luego, diosa.*'

He spoke in rapid dialect to the boat captain, an uncle of his who had been a fairly honest fisherman before he was conscripted into the team, who was not very bright, but who had a non-speaking part which was almost foolproof since he understood no English and hardly any Spanish. Loro cast off the lines which had held the boat to the bank, and the captain started the engine as it began to drift downstream. Loro stood and waved until it vanished around the nearest bend, and then picked up one of the oilcloth packages which had been providently ballasted with a case of rum and plodded towards the next turn upstream, where there was a village of utterly harmless Indians who were always glad to see him and whose daughters were especially hospitable. He would stay there, very pleasantly, until the boat came back for him in a week or two.

Simon stood beside Alice on the narrow deck, gazing silently at the wall of tangled greenery that slid past them until the captain turned the boat in mid-stream, aimed the bow diagonally up towards the bank, cut the engine, and shuffled forward to throw a line over a leaning tree and snub the boat to a berth as nonchalantly as any airline pilot ever made a landing.

The Saint was frowning.

'I seem to be a bit confused,' he said. 'I thought when you came here before you had a lot of native bearers, who got massacred. Then you fought a rear-guard action for two days down the river. And yet we came here all the way from Panama in two days, and Loro is going to make a deal with the headhunters and be back with the golden frogs tomorrow.'

Again she was barely touched by a fleeting uneasiness, but she was ready with the answer.

'Last time, we were exploring. We went off on big swings through the jungle, covering as much ground as we could. We were on one of those hikes when we found the cave. We'd left the boat way down near the mouth of the river. When we fought our way back to it, it was along these banks, only we were on foot. We followed the river because it was the only thing that saved us from getting lost, but you can see what rough going it was.'

('There's a limit to how far we can go with this,' the Professor had said, when he taught her the speech. 'If we gave 'em a full two-week safari, for that kind of money, we'd be almost legitimate.')

Simon nodded uncritically.

'I should have figured that out for myself,' he said. 'It must have been pretty rugged.'

'I'd rather not talk about it,' she said, and meant every word. She despised herself for the palpitation that his unreserved acceptance of her explanation had set at rest again, but she was in no hurry to expose herself to any more potentially devastating questions. 'Shall we try some fishing? Loro says that snook come all the way up here to spawn.'

He was still studying the banks rather than the water, his keen eyes raking along the ragged edge of the forest as though searching for something more than timber and foliage.

'I'd prefer to tramp around on shore a bit, as soon as we've got some lunch under our belts. I wouldn't want to have to go back and say I'd never set foot in this wilderness. We can take the shotgun, and maybe pick up something good to eat.'

She had only her own build-up to thank for his bland assumption that she would not want to be left behind. She thought wildly of all the facile excuses she could make, but she realized that every one of them would have a hollow ring. So far he had only heard talk about her tomboy virtues, and if she seemed to wriggle out of the first opportunity to display them he could hardly help being touched by a flicker of suspicion. And once a man started to doubt, there was no forecasting where his scepticism would turn next.

She gritted her teeth and wished that lightning would strike him, but she forced herself to say: 'That would be fun.'

Four hours later she was nearly ready to strike him down herself. Following the river on foot was a minor nightmare which developed its miseries cumulatively but inexorably until their weight and blackness was smothering.

Sometimes they were stumbling over tangled roots, sometimes sinking above their ankles in thick gluey mud, almost continuously warding off branches, leaves, fronds, vines, and thorns that poked and scratched and tugged at clothing and bare skin. The only respite from that harassment was when they took to the river to circumvent a particularly impassable thicket on land: then there was the treachery of invisible hazards underfoot, the haunting fear of crocodiles, and the discomfort of boots full of water for a memento. Winged and crawling things in infinite variety tickled and hit them. She was soaked with mud up to the hips and with sweat above that; her blonde hair hung in bedraggled skeins. She swore bitterly to herself that if she survived this excursion she would insist on some basic re-writing in her part next time.

The Saint was equally hot and muddy, but his good

humour seemed to feel no strain. He could be fascinated by a sloth which they came upon suspended from a cecropia bough, too sluggish to stir even when he touched it, and he could exclaim delightedly over a toucan taking off before them and speculate earnestly as to why its enormous yellow bill didn't send it immediately into a fatal nose-dive. At other times he seemed to continue seeking for something, picking up a small rock to examine it or taking a handful of loam and gravel from the bank and crumbling it between his fingers, until she had had to ask what he was doing.

'I told you I was a speculator, didn't I, darling? It wasn't only your golden frogs that intrigued me. They suggested something else which you seem to have missed. The ancient frog-worshippers who made 'em had to get the gold from somewhere, and the odds are it wasn't so very far away. Also it isn't likely that they used it all up. If I found the mother lode I'd have a real return on my investment.'

A time came when she felt it would not be worth going any farther for any sort of wealth.

'We should be turning back,' she said, with heroically simulated reluctance. 'We ought to get back to the boat before dark.'

The boat was an old forty-foot native hull on which some intermediate owner had built an oversize deck-house and partitioned it into a crude kind of houseboat; it was cramped and dilapidated and none too clean, but it possessed screens on the windows and a primitive form of shower bath, and from her point of suffering it was starting to resemble a luxury yacht.

The Saint was staring fixedly at the river bank, and suddenly his arm and forefinger stretched out in a compelling gesture.

'Look!'

Her eyes turned where he pointed, and even she saw the metallic yellow gleams on a rock caught by the sun.

He picked up the chunk of stone and wiped it on his shirt. There were half a dozen kernels of the yellow metal embedded in it. He was able to prise one of them out with the point of a pocket knife and lay it in the palm of her hand, a nugget the size of a small pea.

He looked around, and pointed to another rock, and another. All her wretchedness and exhaustion miraculously forgotten, she too began casting around and picked up other stones herself. She discovered that they were surrounded by a score and more of similar half-buried fragments, each crusted with the same crumbs of gold. She found herself grabbing them up wildly, trying to build a stack on one outspread hand and the arm held against her chest.

'Hey, take it easy,' he said, as the top-heavy pile slipped and most of it spilled. 'A couple of souvenirs is enough for now. We'll pick up some more when we come by in the boat, if you like.'

'The boat isn't half *big* enough,' she gasped distractedly.

He was laughing, an almost soundless laughter of celestial contentment.

'Sweetheart, I'm not even thinking about what we could put in that boat. It's what can be taken out with dredger and draglines and strings of barges. This isn't something I'll have to work myself with a pick and shovel.'

'Do you really think it's that big?'

'I know it. I know a lot about mining, among a number of things. This is what every prospector dreams of blundering into. This is the end of the rainbow. When you find this exact kind of geological setup, you know that you haven't a thing to do but file your claim, form a company, and wait for the dividends!'

She trudged all the way back to the boat in a daze that nullified fatigue and time.

'This is one time when a long cold drink isn't going to be

merely medicinal,' he said. 'This will be a legitimate celebration.'

She managed to smile somehow.

'I'd enjoy it lots more if I were clean,' she said. 'Will you save it for me?'

'You've got the best idea. Yell when you're through with the shower, and I'll get clean too. Then we'll make it a party.'

What she wanted more than anything was a chance to gather her wits without the superimposed strain of maintaining a mask. But her usually agile mind seemed to have gone numb. Soap and water, brush and comb, perfume and lipstick, and lastly a minimum of fresh cool garments, made her feel physically better but for once were inadequate to restore her mentally. She was overwhelmed by the magnitude of a complication that had never entered her dizziest dreams.

Later, when he entered the forward section of the deckhouse, which served as both wheelhouse and saloon, Simon Templar found her sitting at the table, her eyes fastened in a hypnotized way on one of the gold-studded pieces of rock which she had brought back.

'A lovely hunk of mineral, isn't it?' he remarked, as he went to work improvising lime and soda and ice with fortification from a bottle of Pimm's Cup which he had thoughtfully contributed to the ship's stores. 'It's a shame you had those headhunters sniping at you the last time you went by there, or I'm sure the Professor would have spotted that formation.'

'But what a wonderful break it was that we asked you to take our picture.'

It was all she could think of to say, a forlorn attempt to be reassured that the foreboding that chilled her to the marrow was unfounded.

He set a tall tinkling glass in front of her, and raised its duplicate to the level of his own lips.

'Here's to Loro,' he said, and drank.

He went on measuring her with a steady gaze, while he put his glass down and placed a cigarette in his mouth.

'Forgive me if I'm off the beam,' he said, 'but a moment ago it sounded just as if you were assuming that we were partners in a newly discovered gold mine.'

'Aren't we?'

'I don't think it's exactly up to you to say that, darling. The only partnership deal we made was that I agreed to finance a highly speculative expedition to try and recover some golden frog idols, with the understanding that if we succeeded I could keep, say, half of them.'

'But if I hadn't brought you here, you'd never have discovered this gold mine,' she was hot-headed enough to argue.

'That's true,' he said coolly. 'And if I hadn't been in the bar at El Panamá I might never have met you – but does that mean the bartender is entitled to cut himself in? I'm a gambler, but I play percentages. I told you this afternoon, even before we found any gold, that it wasn't your frogs I was betting on, but the other angle, the possible gold mine, which I had figured out all by myself. Maybe you could make me feel generous about that, but I'd be uncomfortable if I felt you were grabbing.'

She looked at him speechlessly, and only the most Spartan self-discipline inhibited her from throwing her glass in his face.

He did not appear to notice the gelid malevolence in her eyes, for through her self-inflicted silence his ear was caught and held by a new sound that had been trying to creep in through the thin bulkheads and open screens. He raised a hand, his face suddenly tense and withdrawn.

'Do you hear that?' he asked; and a well-worn behaviour pattern dragged her back rather like an automaton into the script that had been so catastrophically interrupted but which was supposed to be still unreeling itself with her help.

'The drums!' she breathed.

He thrust open the screen door and stepped out on to the scanty triangle of foredeck, and in a moment she followed him. The scrawny captain was already out there, standing rigidly in the bow, with a naked machete gleaming in his hand. Dusk had been falling when Simon and Alice reached the boat, and the brief twilight had long since passed, but now a full moon had risen above the trees and flooded the boat with a cold silver-green brilliance. The river flowed past and under it like a torpidly undulant sheet of liquid lead, but the walls of jungle on each side were by contrast impenetrably black and solid except for the luminous dappling of their topmost foliage. And out of that huge formless obscurity came the monotonous menacing thump and titter of the drums, swelling and fading, shifting and drifting, muttering endless spells and abominations out of the unspeakable night. The tympani virtuosi of the nearby village, inspired by copious libations of Loro's rum, were truly floating it out.

'Sounds like a big fiesta for Loro,' Simon said.

She clutched his arm, to make sure he would feel her shiver.

'No, it's bad,' she said shakily. 'They never play those drums for fun. Only for a blood ritual, a head chopping. I've heard them before – I can never forget . . .'

'Bad,' said the taciturn captain, in corroboration. '*Muy malo!*'

A single ear-splitting shriek pealed out of the blackness, hung quavering on a climax of agony, and was abruptly cut off.

'Oh, no,' Alice sobbed.

At the Saint's first movement, she clung to him tighter.

'No, I won't let you. There's nothing you could do!'

Like a giant firefly, a torch blinked alight in the forest, flaring and eclipsing as it wandered among the trees. It was joined by another, and another, until there were six or seven of them shimmering and weaving towards the river, throwing weirdly moving silhouettes of deformed tree trunks and twisted jungle growth. The drums came nearer, picked up a more feverish tempo.

As the torches bobbed closer to the bank, they revealed not only the shapes of the brown men who carried them, but the gleaming leaping forms of a horde of other naked creatures that writhed and capered around them. The male population of the village where Loro sojourned didn't do things by halves. He had explained to them that this was what the incomprehensible white tourists expected, and in return for the rum which he dispensed they were always ready to oblige. It was more fun for them than a square dance, anyway.

Then, as if at a signal, the torches drew together and became almost still. And in the midst of them, on the point of a spear, to an accompaniment of shrill yips and yells, was raised a bleeding human head.

This was Professor Humphrey Nestor's crowning inspiration, the climactic triumph of his dramatic genius. The head, moulded in papier-mâché from a plaster matrix which the Professor had made himself, was a recognizable facsimile of Loro's to pass at that distance and in the flickering torchlight, and the long black hair affixed to its scalp and the gold ring in one ear were clinchers of identification. The ketchup which dripped from its neck was a gruesome touch of realism which had become even more horrifyingly effective when some of the performers had discovered how good it tasted and had taken to dipping their fingers in the drips and licking them with ghoulish glee. Thus the subsidizer of the whole elaborate fraud was to be fully and incontrovertibly convinced that Loro was dead, the guns were lost, the expedition had failed, and there was nothing left but to kiss his investment goodbye and be thankful his own head was still on his shoulders. At that, he would go home with an anecdote to embroider for the rest of his life which in itself was almost worth the capital outlay, which he could take as a tax deduction, if he could get anyone to believe him.

Alice screamed.

All the torches went out as if a switch had been pulled. It had been found too dangerous to leave them alight any longer than it took to fulfil their purpose. One earlier victim had been so emotionally affected that he had fetched a gun and started blazing away, and might easily have hurt someone.

Out of the darkness that seemed to swallow the land again came a rustle like unseen wings, and a shower of arrows plonked into the bulkheads and the deck. They were shot by the best archers in the village, who could be relied on not to hit anyone accidentally.

The captain let out a yell of fear, and his machete flashed, cutting the bow rope by which they were moored with a single stroke. Instantly the boat started to move with the strong deep current. The captain scuttled into the wheel-house, and as Simon instinctively dragged Alice down to the deck they heard the laboured grinding of the electric starter. The air quivered with bloodcurdling ululations from the Stygian shoreline. After four excruciating attempts the engine finally caught and the boat came under control; turning with increasing sureness out towards the centre of the river. Another shower of arrows fell mostly in the water behind them, and the hysterical war-whoops faded rapidly as the boat gathered speed with the stream.

Simon rose and helped Alice up, and sympathetically let her continue to hold on to him since that was what she seemed to want.

'It's all my fault,' she moaned. 'I got Loro killed, and lost you all that money—'

'Loro got himself killed,' said the Saint sternly. 'It was his own idea, and he was sure he could get away with it. Nobody was twisting his arm. As for the money, I don't know what you think I've got to complain about.'

She had to force herself to recall how radically inappropriate half of her carefully rehearsed speech had become in the light of the veritable catastrophe which had intervened.

The boat, driving at full throttle down the stream which the climbing moon had turned into a floodlit highway, must already have been somewhere near the place which they had reached so laboriously that afternoon on foot. Simon pointed towards the now silent blackness of the land.

'I'm not an archaeologist, and I'll be satisfied with what's there,' he said. 'I'll be back with all the machinery necessary to get it out, and all the men that are needed – armed, if they have to be – to chase those headhunters away. Before long, the headhunters'll probably have been scared so far off into the hills that you won't have any trouble getting back into your frog cave. I'll get along all right until then. I've still got that prospecting concession for this river – remember?'

5

'It was, literally, like an answer to prayer,' said Professor
Humphrey Nestor piously. 'As you know, Mr Tombs – I'm
sure I must have mentioned it – I was scheduled to stop over
to deliver a special lecture on Inca mythology at the University
of Miami. So I had asked Michigan to forward my mail for a
few days in care of the President. That is how I happened to
receive this letter from the executors of this rich uncle from
whom I frankly never expected to inherit so much as an old
encyclopedia.'

He handed Simon the unfolded letter. It was nicely
typed on a letterhead purporting to be that of a firm of
New York attorneys, and informed Professor Humphrey
Nestor that they were holding at his disposal a legacy of
fifty thousand dollars from the estate of Hannibal Nestor,
deceased, and would appreciate his instructions regarding
delivery of the same.

Simon glanced at it and handed it back with a smile of
congratulation. Nobody could esteem the value of an efficiently faked document higher than he.

'That's simply wonderful,' he said whole-heartedly.

'Naturally,' said the Professor, 'all I could think of was to
get the money as quickly as possible and return here while we
were still hot on the scent, as you might say, of those golden
frogs.'

'Naturally.'

'Getting the money was only a matter of formality. Then I

wired Alice, and took the next plane back here after my lecture. Of course, by that time you had already left on your ill-fated trip. No doubt you can imagine my feelings when she was forced to tell me the whole story. It would be impossible for me to forgive the bargain she made with you if I did not realize how altruistic although misguided her motives were. But both of us will always bear on our souls the burden of the death of poor faithful Loro.'

He bowed his head; and a subdued Alice, becomingly garbed in black, meekly followed suit.

'Don't blame yourselves too much,' said the Saint. 'I've already told her—'

The Professor raised his hand.

'Let us not discuss it,' he said. 'All I ask, for my own-satisfaction and peace of mind, is that you should permit me to reimburse you for your loss. Call it conscience money, or blood money, as you will. And let us consider that iniquitous compact ended, as if it had never been made.'

He took another piece of paper from his pocket and held it out to the Saint. Simon took it, and saw that it was a cashier's cheque for ten thousand dollars which his practised eye told him was certainly not forged.

'If you put it that way, Professor,' he said, respectfully, 'I hardly see how I can refuse.'

'I understand you will not be a loser, in any event. May I ask what you are proposing to do about your lucky find?'

'I haven't had time to do anything much yet,' said the Saint. 'In fact, for the present I'm keeping it right under my hat, and as you know I've asked Alice to do the same. I don't want some local hotshots getting wind of it and maybe pulling some fast legal shenanigans before everything's sewn up. I have got an attorney forming a local corporation, which will have quite a nominal capital, most of which I'll put up myself – about a hundred grand. For operating capital, I'll get a loan from some Texas oil men I know; in that way, the value of the original stock will skyrocket much faster as soon as we get going, and I can take a nice capital gain instead of paying a ninety per cent income tax.'

The Professor nodded.

'Alice tells me she had some misunderstanding with you about the legal and moral rights to your mining claim. She was absolutely wrong, of course—'

'I know it now,' Alice said contritely. 'I was very stupid, and I apologize.'

'But,' said the Professor, 'we do have a friendly interest in your venture. Your opening up of the country should eventually make it possible for us to get back to our frogs again – if they are still there. And I do claim that we contributed something, however indirectly, to your good fortune. Here I am, Mr Tombs, with what is left of this legacy, and very little knowledge of financial matters. I would like to invest something that would bring in a good return and enable me to continue my researches. Alice and I have been so close to this, and we have the best reasons to believe in it. I would like to ask you – not as a right, but as a favour – if you would consider letting us in on the ground floor.'

'How much would you want to invest?' Simon asked in a businesslike manner.

The Professor looked appealingly at Alice. She opened her purse, and then a billfold from it, and took out five cashier's cheques, each made out simply to Bearer. It was the most liquid and compact way she had been able to think of to carry her retirement fund. She put one of them back, and handed Simon the other four. Each of them was made out for five thousand dollars.

'I told him we could speculate this much,' she said.

Simon looked at them judicially.

'I was only a little peeved because I thought Alice was

jumping the gun,' he said. 'When you put it this way, I couldn't be mean enough to refuse. But I can't take all this – it would be against a foolish principle of mine.'

He gave her back two of the cheques and put the other two away in his wallet.

'I'll give you a receipt,' he said.

He fetched a sheet of paper and wrote on it:

Received from Professor Humphrey Nestor, and Alice Nestor, the sum of $10,000 (*Ten Thousand Dollars*) *in return for which I promise to issue them stock to the same par value in the Golden Frog Mining Corporation, as soon as it is available.*

Probably, he reflected, a smart lawyer could prove that such an indefinite promise was not even fraudulent. Not that the Saint intended to wait around even another twelve hours to find out.

'Will that do?' he asked.

They looked pathetically grateful and yet somewhat disappointed, so that he rather regretted the quixotic impulse that had compelled him to refuse half their money. But he felt that he had been well repaid for the time he had spent preparing that elegant 'licence' for himself. As for the preliminary trip over the river, on which his Navy friend had flown him from Coco Solo and helped him dump several sackfuls of carefully salted rock, the plane and the gas had been unwittingly supplied by Uncle Sam, and the trip had been purely a joyride. The Nestors, he thought, should be taught a lesson to be more circumspect about working a routine with so many transparent fabrications in it, but they had certainly put on a first-class production, and the Saint did not want to be too cruel.

Watch for the sign of the Saint!

If you have enjoyed this Saintly adventure, look out for the other Simon Templar novels by Leslie Charteris – all available in print and ebook from Mulholland Books